101 67 1347 (12.06) 18.73

The Farm Dog

The Farm Dog

A. R. Lloyd

CENTURY

LONDON MELBOURNE AUCKLAND JOHANNESBURG

For Dora

First published in Great Britain in 1986 by
Century Hutchinson Ltd,
Brookmount House, 62–65 Chandos Place,
Covent Garden, London WC2N 4NW

Century Hutchinson Publishing Group (Australia) Pty Ltd
16–22 Church Street, Hawthorn, Melbourne, Victoria 3122

Century Hutchinson (NZ) Ltd
32–34 View Road, PO Box 40-086, Glenfield, Auckland 10

Century Hutchinson Group (SA) Pty Ltd
PO Box 337, Bergvlei 2012, South Africa

Set in Plantin

Printed and bound in Great Britain by
Anchor Brendon Ltd, Tiptree, Essex.

ISBN 0 7126 9513 3

Part One

DUNKIRK

1

The man raised the pointed bar and plunged it vertically downwards. It pierced the clod and he worked it. The ground was firm. He wrenched outwards in circles to make the hole wider. Again, he lifted the tool, shooting back at the opening. With each lunge, the hole deepened.

Bursts of squally rain lashed him. He shoved a stake in the breach. Ramming it home with a mallet, he paced a gap then raised the pitcher. The row of chestnut pales lengthened, open-spaced up the meadow. The figure toiled at the fencing with bleak ferocity.

In the hedge, the dog shivered. He was thin, with staring ribs and his tired, watchful eyes watered. The wind raked, blowing cruelly from the north, searing grass, slicing scrub like a bill hook. The dog watched the farmer. The bar plunged; the mallet swung and impacted.

Chill clouds scudded. Across a vaporous sky-wall, rooks formed straggling columns between naked copses. Jackdaws boosted their numbers, but the wind drowned their rumpus. At last the man grasped his knapsack, the dog squirming closer. The stray could smell the hot thermos and the food with it. Salivating, he crouched in the hedgerow, weak and ravenous.

Wilf Tuck grunted. Still sweating, he had folded a sack on which to squat in the lee, another sack round his shoulders. His pale gaze met the dog's. 'What's this, then?' He had the eye of a stockman. 'Damme, *you're* a poor beggar, scarcely fit for the knacker.'

He tore a crust of bread roughly. The dog snapped as Tuck flicked it. 'Christ,' the man said through his raw wind-chafed stubble, 'you'd rob me.' He poured the tea down his gullet then lobbed more of the bread. A shard of cheese followed.

The dog pushed his nose forward but drew back when Tuck shifted. A coarse, collie-type mongrel, he was unsure of the farmer. 'Please yourself,' the man grunted. Screwing the cap on the thermos, he rose and the dog sniffed for leavings. 'You'll not fatten on crumbs. Now get home – if you've got one. I've a field to fence, damn you.'

He strung the empty sacks round him. Picking up a wrench, the farmer bent to the weather, straining wire to the brace posts and battering staples. The barbs on the wire tore him. He strove, ignoring the bleeding. 'B'God,' he rasped, looking up, 'you still there? Clear off, like I told you.'

The mongrel cringed, his eyes sullen. The wind combed his nape, mauling ears that were already sodden. Rooks had settled to roost and a steely light glimmered, casting Tuck in harsh outline. The hammer blows thudded. Stubbornly, the dog lingered with a half-hope of succour. Instinct held him to the man – to the lone drudging figure – until dark, when Tuck vanished. Then the dog, skulking forward, put his snout down.

He dogged the trail to the farmhouse. There were chinks in the black-out, revealing gutters that leaked and a muddy yard broom. The man's spoor was powerful. The dog scratched the door, whining. For a while nothing happened, then a bolt eased, a gap opened and he shot in like the devil. The light and warmth stunned him.

'What's happening?' the woman's voice was abrasive. 'What's going on through there, Tuck, in the name of heaven?'

The lamp burned with a faint odour. A dresser rose to the ceiling, bills and oddments set on it: an old veterinary manual, a wood-cased wireless and battery. Knitting lay on an armchair. Logs blazed in the fireplace.

The dog crouched in a corner. He had grown weak seeking shelter and was going no farther. They could do what they wanted. The dog was damp, sore and hungry, but warm for the moment. 'A bag of bones,' huffed the woman. 'What a mess,' she protested.

'Name of Zac on his collar.'

Zac surveyed the fire sharply. Flames leaped in the ingress, a sappy log whistling. Sparks starred the black cavern. The fierce core of heat frightened. It stirred alarm in the mongrel but the flicking rays thawed and he welcomed the comfort. Tuck's gun spanned the firebreast. 'No address,' the man added.

'We're not keeping him, Tuck.'

'Go on, fill him a bowl, Rose.'

'For tonight – then he's going.'

She put the bowl in the kitchen, on the bricks by the stove. The stove was black, its knob silvery. The dog ate like a shark, lips curled back, his teeth snapping. Tuck's wife grunted. 'The brute's starving.' She put her hands on her hips, saying, 'I'm not keeping a house dog. He can stop for tonight, Tuck.'

The door closed and Zac was left in the darkness as their voices receded.

'He's no pup.'

'Pushing on, like us, woman.'

'And tomorrow he's going.'

The dog whimpered.

Zac was sore – sore from the heath and the forest, from days and nights spent in wandering. Each hour had seemed colder; each mile, more painful. He had come from the mists, from the morass and the nightmare it harboured. He scratched as his coat dried. A grey cat watched, its eyes hostile.

The kitchen was spartan. Eggs stood in buckets, to be scrubbed in the morning.

The dog pawed the door latch. The door swung and his nose quested. The man and his wife had gone up, leaving downstairs in shadow. Zac explored the back passage. Shabby coats and hats hung there, and a brace of harled

3

rabbits, blood dry on their noses. He had stopped feeling hungry.

On the floor, there were boots. The dark tunnel was narrow, shored up by rail sleepers as a shelter from air raids. So far, there had been none; just a few scouting aircraft. 'A phoney war,' Wilf Tuck called it. The dog reached the staircase. He could hear the couple above and returned to the parlour.

They had let down the black-out. The night had stilled. Now a frost rimed the windows; owls fluted. But the room remained warm. It held chairs and a table, an old handle-wound gramophone, candles set among nick-nacks and socks left for darning. The dog flopped at the fireside. A searchlight shafted. He saw its beam through iced glass, then the pale finger vanished.

He must have slept. The room was suddenly smoky and he saw the mat burning. The fumes were dense, like the bog mist. In the mist had dwelled terror. Zac coughed, his eyes stinging. He was frightened now, barking. Running back to the stairs, he barked again, his voice urgent.

The smoke was on its way up as Tuck, choking, groped down. He wore boots and pyjamas. Zac could hear the boots stamping. Ducking into the passage, the mongrel dog listened. 'It's the mat,' Tuck was gasping, 'I've caught the beggar in time but there's smoke to the ceiling.'

His wife's voice was accusing. 'You never made the fire safe, Tuck.'

'Well, it's safe now, by God. Two more minutes, we'd have been roasted.'

'It's that dog – a bad omen.'

'Damn it, woman, he woke us!'

'Aye,' the woman admitted, 'give the devil his due, he did that for us.'

The dog ran into the morning. Cold air struck him. The grey house stood back bleakly against the icy dawn sky. Yet he relished the frost now that there was good food in his belly. Tuck's wife had relented. 'You need fattening, poor beggar.

Mind – you're still on probation.' Rooting on, he put Tuck's dungheap rooster to noisy flight.

'Be still, damn you!'

Tuck was humping hay to the midden. The great fork-loads straggled, engulfing his shoulders. Steers were jostling, breath steaming. There was ice on their trough. He smashed through with his heel and dipped a bucket, then made his way to the farm truck. Filling the radiator, he cranked the engine.

The mongrel waited.

'Christ!' Tuck bellowed.

He jumped back, his wrist flapping. He swung again; there was a cough. The engine fired at the third swing and Tuck snatched the throttle. The bonnet bounced, the cab rattled. 'Come on, damn you.' The farmer held the door open. 'Get in – don't waste time.'

Hunched forward, Tuck drove like a ploughman, grinding the gears of the old Morris. As he did so, he muttered, his lips blue with cold, speaking more to himself than to Zac, who sat upright. 'In the house, *she's* the master. That's Rule One to remember. Out here, I'm the gaffer.' They lurched and swayed between hedges. 'Rule Two – damn the Wilsons. Damn all tinkers and their ponies.'

Air lashed through the windows. The dog snuffled the slipstream, his ears flat, the frost stinging. The lane's verges were hoary, the fields rimed and hard-frozen. Lapwings dotted the plough-swell, each standing one-legged, the other leg drawn up beneath it. Zac lurched. Tuck was hacking the brakes on, his big raw face stormy.

'There's the beggars.' Five rough ponies were grazing amid the winter corn. 'That's the damned Wilsons for you – leave their nags on my wheat!'

Tuck got out, his arms waving. 'Go on, dog, shift the devils. Now we'll see what you're made of.'

He began to run, shouting. Catching his mood, Zac raced forward, his coat dark on the iced field, neck stretched and tail streaming. There was tan and fawn in his colour, and some white, but the black dominated. He moved like a shadow. Now the ponies were jogging, heads high, nostrils flaring.

'Go on, hound, fetch them out!'

Zac barked, and the lively, fleet steeds from the forest began to canter. The biggest one was cobby, a truculent skewbald, and the dog went for his fetlock. A sharp kick sent Zac sprawling. Springing up, he charged back, pushing the steeds down the hedge to the gate Tuck had opened. Their hooves rang on the lane's surface.

'Hi-yi!' the man hollered. He dived back to the truck. 'Get aboard – now we'll run them! Now we'll warm their feet for them!'

Zac was on the seat, panting. He licked his bruises. The big farmer glanced sideways. 'Rule Three – if there's hooves on the beggar, watch its backside!'

He gunned the truck and they roared behind the ponies. The beasts took off at a gallop, hotfoot for the heath. Tuck drove like a demon. 'Giddup!' he bawled madly. He was steering with one hand, head and shoulders through the window, free hand drubbing the door panel. 'Hiyi-yi, giddup, dammit!'

The stampede careered wildly. Bucking, plunging, the animals pounded, their clatter resounding. The truck swerved behind them. Frosted grit whipped the windscreen; steam gushed from the bonnet. Between hedgerows, the lathered steeds thundered; between walls and farm fences – over crossings, down hills and through hamlets.

'Hiyi-yi!'

Thump, thump, thump!

Zac was barking, his snout in the slipstream. The dog was elated. Past haystacks, they rattled; past barns and pillboxes, and the raking grey barrels of Bofors guns on ack-ack platforms. At last, the chill landscape widened and the trail disgorged on the heath. Zac braced himself as the truck stopped. The steeds had fanned through the gorse, no longer channelled by hedges. Blown, they stood off and snorted.

'Come on, dog.' Tuck got down. They were close to a hutment and three men came forward. Their clothes were thin, their knotted scarves flimsy. Blue-jowled, they looked frozen. Tuck faced them, his fists clenched. 'You owe me,' he told them.

'Not us,' said one tinker.

'They're not ours,' said another, 'they're wild ponies, mister.'

'Shod?' snarled Tuck.

Feet apart, he stood glaring, his battered cap slanted. 'I could sell them. Next time, I'll impound them and sell them. Then we'll know whose they are, friend.'

'You'll not do that.' The men advanced. Zac was bristling. 'You do that, there'll be trouble.'

'Trouble?' Tuck said, his fists stirring. 'You're *always* damned trouble. Don't threaten *me*, tinker.'

The three crowded the farmer. The dog could smell their resentment, the incipient violence. Head low, he inched forward, teeth obtrusive. 'Keep your cur away, mister.' Now the men shuffled backwards. 'We know that dog from the forest. He's no good. He'll not profit you, that one.'

Zac watched them, eyes glinting.

'Stay away,' Tuck harangued them, 'just keep off my acres.' And, as they retreated, 'You want trouble, you'll get it – by God, you'll get trouble.' He strode to the wagon. Across his shoulder, he called, 'Come back, dog, leave the beggars.'

Driving home, Tuck scowled fiercely. 'No bloody good, aren't you?' He opened the throttle and they hurtled round corners. He eyed the stray mongrel. 'I'll tell you what *I* think – you know a rogue when you see one. That'll do to go on with. You stick with Tuck.'

2

'He's a puzzlement,' Rose said.

'He scared the Wilsons,' Tuck told her.

'I'd like to know where he came from.'

Wilf Tuck cleaned his shotgun. The woman was knitting. Turning up the Aladdin, she frowned in the lamplight. The dog drowsed, sprawled between them. 'He's not young,' Tuck asserted, 'but there's herding dog in him.'

'And the rest,' Rose said dourly. She kept her eyes on the stitches as the broad needles rattled. At last, she stretched out the garment, a drab Balaclava. 'For Roy – the cold nights on duty.'

'France,' the man said, disgruntled. He fixed a brush on the rod and pumped at the barrels. Smoothing oil on the metal, he said, 'Damn the army. Roy in France – where's the reason? He should be on the farm. The farm's more important.'

Rose hitched wool with a finger. 'He could've stayed,' she said calmly, reconciled as Tuck would not be. 'He could've had an exemption and stayed to farm. He was cussed. He's got your cussedness, Roy has.'

'Let us down,' Tuck said harshly. He snapped the breech of the twelve-bore. 'Went off when he was needed.' The man's voice was a rumble. He said slowly, head shaking, 'I never thought he would do it, leave the farm ...'

'There's a war on.'

'War be damned,' said the farmer. He stretched, replacing the shotgun. 'It won't last beyond summer.'

'Then he'll return.'

The man grunted. Needles clicked.

'Maybe you're right,' he said gruffly, and went out with the mongrel.

'Just take care,' called the woman. 'Those Wilsons bear malice. Just you mind they're not snooping.'

'I've the dog,' Tuck responded.

The night air was frosty. He flashed a torch into byres where huddled weaners were sleeping, then lit a lamp in the stable. The horses turned their heads slowly, their shadows hurled to the hayloft like dinosaurs rising. It was warm and the stalls were tangy with urine.

Tuck worked with a shovel. 'Damn the army,' he groused, clearing dung from the bedding. 'Gid' over!' He filled hayracks, still mumbling. 'There's work here – more important. Blast the boy, he's a farmer.' He doused the lamp. Calling the dog, he left the stable.

In the dark, a sheep bleated. The chill stabbed the mongrel and he ran, his nose working. Rabbits scuffled from verges; roosting birds moved in hedges; a stoat had passed, its musk heavy. Zac could hear the man cussing. 'Driving bloody Bren-carriers! He could drive that old Case so she purred like a kitten.'

The Case stood on the ploughland. It had metal-toothed wheels, unfitted for roadwork. In the murk, the teeth bristled. As Zac advanced to the tractor, two men left its shadow, bent low, thin scarves streaming. The can they dropped scattered fuel and the air reeked of the liquid.

'I'll have them,' Tuck shouted. 'Draining my engines – I'll have them!'

But they outran the farmer.

Zac chased one to the fence, where the man turned, lashing his boot. It caught the dog on the neck. He let the culprit escape him and shook as the blow started throbbing. He was not new to such treatment. Their huts were the first place he had reached on leaving the forest, lost and hungry. They had driven him off then with oaths and kicks.

The team topped the brow slowly and came on through the mizzle. Its progress was lugubrious. The horses strained; the man plodded. The soil balled on Tuck's boots and he lurched, shoulders tilting. His voice urged and steadied, while Zac watched.

Now, Tuck halted the horses, yanking on the plough

handles, then pressed on, with the team champing. Back and forth, it seemed endless. At the headlands, he paused, for the horses to rest. Then on they laboured, blurred by the raw precipitation, the shroud of a day that had died at dawn.

Zac grew restive. Pushing wetly through a hedge, he saw the tractor draw up and Steve dismount from it. He was wearing two topcoats, with reaper twine round the middle. Tuck's tractorman tinkered with the machine. 'Had enough of horse ploughing?' He looked up, his hands greasy. 'The boss works the hard way.'

The young man tapped the Case. 'Should run sweeter. She's the workhorse for me, Zac. I understand tractors. So did Roy. The old man's a dunce with them.' He stooped to the engine. Gulls dived, snatching worms and dis-embowelling small rodents the plough had made homeless. A pair of crows foraged. 'The boss understands livestock, knows all about cattle.' Steve mused aloud. 'Knows damn all about tractors.'

It was the day of the mechanic. Steve looked up at the seagulls. That was the place to be now, aloft with the Air Force, your boots clean and shining! He climbed back on the Case. The damp bucket-seat juddered. 'Mind your tail, dog,' he shouted.

Zac moved on to the sheep-fold. In the haze, ewes were coughing. The odour was powerful. He reached the first set of hurdles. The sheep were on roots, and the ground was trampled and muddy; it stank of foul vegetation. Zac could still hear the tractor, but kept his gaze on Tuck's shepherd.

'Be gone,' the man rasped, his old voice wheezing. He was wrapped in sacking and his shuffling feet squelched. On his back there were hurdles, transfixed by a fold-bar.

Zac considered the sheepdogs – dog and bitch, a rugged pair. A dead sheep lay before them, struck down by the staggers. Now, ripping the belly, they tore at its innards and gorged.

'Be gone, damn you!'

'You're on time,' said the woman. At the house, he was

welcome. 'More than Tuck is,' Rose told him. The place smelled of cooking. She put his bowl by the stove, and Zac was eating when Steve called. The lad brought the milk-can.

'Where's the boss?' Tuck's wife asked.

'He won't be long,' Steve responded. 'It's too dark now for ploughing.'

'For Tuck?'

Steve looked solemn. He admired Tuck's old woman; the boss took some handling. Rose was firm – tough but comely – and she awed Steve. He had seen her run from a mouse and cradle lambs while she fed them. All the same, Rose could skin you.

'True,' he promised, 'he's back with the horses. He'll be in when he's fed them.'

'And done six *more* jobs,' Rose said. She inspected the cookpots. 'Tuck'll kill himself working.'

'He misses Roy,' Steve asserted.

'He's got you.' The young man was a worker; they were lucky to have him. 'I'll give you a tip, Steve – if ever you marry, be punctual for meals. It'll save you a basting.'

Steve grinned. 'I'll remember. Best get off to my digs, then.'

The dog licked the bowl clean. Rose half-filled it with milk and he tongued the rich liquor just drawn from Tuck's shorthorns. Zac's tail signalled pleasure. Steve had pulled the door open. Cold air swept the kitchen. Rose bawled, 'Close it!'

Steve stood in the doorway.

'Mrs Tuck, come and listen.'

'Sounds like thunder.'

'That's gunfire.' They were standing in shadow, Rose screening the oil lamp. Abruptly, searchlights were shining, crisscrossing the sky-wall.

Rose said, 'Best get on home, Steve.'

She went to the oven. Zac was close, his eyes rolling. Rose attended to her cooking. 'All right, dog!' she said fiercely. 'Damn Tuck, always working; never here when you want him. What's that?'

11

The door opened, and Tuck and Steve came in quickly. The guns were loud. A Bofors fired on the heath, shaking windows. Tuck said, 'Into the passage.' He had reached for the twelve-bore and they stood in the shelter, damp coats hanging round them. 'They'll scare the bloody sheep, damn them.'

'German engines,' Steve muttered. 'Hear the throb.'

It came nearer. The dog was trembling. Powerful engines pulsated. There was no longer any gunfire, just the roar of the aircraft, coming closer and lower. Then the plane had shot over and, in the tense quiet which followed, Zac's panting was strident. Next instant, the house rocked.

'Bombs,' breathed Steve.

Rose clutched Tuck. 'Lord, the buildings!'

Tuck went out. 'They've gone, damn them.' The night was strangely unruffled. Only the pheasants were calling. Their cacophony echoed. On the westerly airstream, an acrid smell wafted, but the buildings were standing.

'Thank the Lord,' said the woman.

'I'll check the dairy herd,' Steve said.

'Never mind,' Tuck directed, 'the cows won't be bothered. Go and steady the horses. You stay inside, woman, and keep the doors bolted. There may be men – if the plane crashed. I'll look round with the mongrel.'

'Tuck ...' But Tuck had departed, gun cocked, his eyes narrow.

Zac ran on through the shadows. The lane filled with movement. It seemed alive, like a river, a great patter swelling, as shapes rose, surged and jostled. The sheep burst on him headlong, the flock in blind panic, its fold hurdles flattened. Tuck threw open a field gate. 'Turn them, Zac. Turn the beggars!'

Zac raced back, snarling, snapping.

Wool tore as he tussled, hurling himself at the leaders. The ewes heaved in their terror. Tuck was in the road, bawling. At last, the vanguard was diverted, and the flock was steered to the enclosure. Soon, the sheepdogs loomed darkly and Zac heard the shepherd, his thin whistle skirling.

'Where'd they fall?'

'On yon furrows ...'

Tuck barged on without waiting. At first he kept to the lane then, shoving through thickets, he surveyed the black ploughland. Now, the pheasants had settled. A shadowy hare fled. The acrid odour was trenchant as man and dog searched in silence.

Zac's snout was probing. He stopped at the Case. Tuck shone a torch on it. The tractor was safe and they advanced. The air was biting. A tall pole broke the skyline, leaning crazily sideways with cables strewn round it.

Zac drew back, his growl chesty. A vast hole lay before him, the size of Tuck's parlour, and two more holes beyond it. 'B'God,' the man muttered. His torch lit the crater, which still smelled of burning.

But already, at the bottom, a clay porridge had gathered where smashed land-drains trickled. It resembled a cesspit. 'God-damned war,' rasped the farmer. 'Roy's gone, my land's pitted. All I've gained is a mongrel.' He eyed the dog. 'A stray mongrel!'

3

'He'll be claimed.'

'Maybe,' Steve said.

The dog was news in the village.

'If he's so smart,' said the blacksmith, 'there'll be somebody looking.'

Steve tossed Zac a hoof-paring. Tuck's team shook their nosebags. The horses stamped, munching quietly. Steve had brought them for shoeing, the dog loping with them. Now, Zac chewed the paring.

Steve yawned. Rutter bored him – and the smith's grimy workshop: sweat, cinders and horse dung. The blacksmith's steady rhythm tried the young farmhand's patience. Tractors needed less fussing.

The smith plied his hammer. His stature was stumpy, his forearm broad-corded. He spat. 'Someone's a loser.'

Steve's gaze sought the village. There was not much to Murton: forge, pub, road to Ringwood. The church was damp, like his lodgings; Doc Benson's house, peeling. The place was weathered as fell rock. There had once been a signpost, slim and white in the tansy, but that, with all Britain's signposts, had been removed 'for the duration'.

'Mind you,' said the blacksmith, 'a stray dog can travel. He could've been bombed from somewhere.' He stooped to fit the shoe, and the hoof sizzled. 'Whoa, hoss!' Rutter coaxed. Then it was finished and he straightened.

A van stopped at the curb. The thin-featured man inside mouthed a stained cigarette-end, his eyes on the mongrel.

Steve said, 'Tuck won't part easy.'

'Obstinate,' said the blacksmith. 'All the Tucks are strong-headed – Roy, away in the army; Di, his sister, in London. There's a girl with a will!'

Steve had not met the daughter. He said, 'You know Roy's in France now?'

'Away from his father. The boy's independent.'

And in uniform, Steve thought. Driving better than tractors! He heard the van go. Its tappets rattled, he noted. He said, 'I'd not join the army. If I enlist I'll be flying – aircrew,' he determined. 'That's the service I fancy.'

'Oh yes?' Rutter was teasing. 'You're the man for Tuck's girl then: a pair of high fliers!' But Steve was not listening, his mind far over Murton, where the granite-hued cloud rose. His thoughts were still soaring as he took the team homeward, riding one, leading two, the dog jogging beside him.

Zac went back to the farmer. The big man was ditching. He threw the sharp-edged spade fiercely. The van had stopped near the buildings and the driver alighted. For a while, he took stock, then, discarding a Woodbine, closed the door and snooped forward.

His blue suit was shiny. He trod with quick, prying movements, light shoes placed discreetly, ill-suited to yard muck. A shed disgorged feathers as he opened the door. Rose was plucking for market and soft flurries drifted.

'Tuck about?' asked the thin man.

Rose looked up, deep in plumage. She wore hat, coat and gumboots. 'Tuck?' The woman ripped briskly. Dead fowls were strewn round her. 'When did Tuck pluck a chicken?' The chore made Rose vicious. 'Down the lane, man. He's digging.'

This time, Zac saw the van halt.

'Gaffer Tuck?' asked the stranger.

'Aye.' The farmer kept working. Clay flew as he shovelled.

'About the dog ...'

The spade grated. 'I'm a busy man, mister.' Tuck shed sweat for his living. All his life, he had laboured, toiled to husband his acres. He did not stop for travellers.

'I'll take the dog then and leave you.'

Tuck examined his ditching, the pitch and smoothness of sides, the plane through topsoil to subsoil. He took a pride in his efforts. He chopped again, slicing deeply. The old ditch

15

had got shallow and soon filled in a downpour; the new would carry Noah's flood.

He said, 'And what dog would that be?'

'The mongrel.'

Zac brooded. He had his head on his forepaws.

Tuck sniffed, saying nothing. The air was dank. It hung closely. Pigeons' wings clapped like gunshots. Beneath a dour hedgerow-oak, gnats had started to swarm and the other, his lips dry, said, licking them quickly, 'Name of Zac – dog's been missing,'

'Oh, yes?' Tuck said slowly.

'Stroke of luck I was passing.' The man's eyes were artful. He brushed off a feather. 'I heard in Murton you'd found him.'

The spade hit a tree-root.

'Ah,' Tuck murmured.

'They told me ...'

'That the mongrel was useful, worth a bob or two, doubtless?'

'Always was,' sneered the stranger.

He eyed the dog and Zac glowered.

The farmer hacked the obstruction. He had not paused. No one stopped Wilf Tuck working. He had toiled through the depression, when agriculture was bankrupt; pigs had failed and corn was worthless. The big man had reared cattle. Staking all on a herd, he had seen milk touch the bottom – fourpence ha'penny a gallon.

Somehow, Tuck had survived and held on to his acres. No one cheated the farmer – of his land or a mongrel. He had not worked to be cheated; had not toiled and kept toiling, as now he toiled with the spade, despising the liar.

'Can you prove he's yours?' Tuck said.

'He's not *yours*.'

'Try,' Tuck challenged. For a moment he rested. 'Go on, man, take the beggar. Here, put this on his collar.' He drew some twine from a pocket. 'Put that on him,' he goaded.

'Right,' the stranger responded. Zac looked up, his eyes like forge coals. The man hesitated. He stretched the twine, his glance chary. 'Right,' he said, 'we'll be off, then.'

String in hand, he stepped forward. Zac was still as a reptile. The man was growing less certain. 'Right ...' He stooped to the collar, then jerked back, his mouth gaping. The dog was clamped to his arm. As he tugged, Zac's jaws tightened.

'Get him off!'

'Your dog?' Tuck said.

'Christ's sake,' the man blurted.

'That'll do, Zac, give over.'

Tuck took hold of the impostor. The farmer's fists forced him backwards, yanking him up so his legs dragged. He was thrust through the hedge, Zac still growling beside them. The van stood in the lane, and Tuck stuffed the man in it. 'That'll do, dog, he's leaving.'

Later, Tuck took his cap off. He scratched his head. '*Someone* owns you!'

4

Hawthorn blossomed. Sun splashed the chalk uplands but the forest was shadowed. Great storm anvils menaced. Steve arrived at the platform as the steam train departed. 'Miss Tuck?' He was doubtful. On the small, smutty station, the girl looked too dressy.

Only her stride – loose-limbed like a landsman's – offset his misgivings until, as the smoke cleared, her strong face reassured him.

'You'll be Steve.' The girl eyed him. She kept hold of her suitcase, ignoring his raised hand, and her gaze ranged to the dog. 'So you're the welcoming party?'

'Me and Zac, I'm afraid . . .'

She said crisply, 'Don't tell me – Tuck's flogging his guts out and Ma's plucking chickens.'

'They'll be real pleased to see you.'

'They'll be pleased,' said Tuck's daughter. 'If I were Roy, they'd be *real* pleased. They're used to *my* absence.'

'In London?'

'I work there.' She slung her bag on the farm truck. 'I'll drive,' she commanded.

'In *those* shoes?' She was Tuck's girl!

'In these shoes!' Her eyes glinted. 'Get in, I shan't smash it.' In the cab, the dog nosed her. 'God,' she laughed, her teeth brilliant, 'he's as worried as you are. Suppose he's a *man's* dog?'

'He's your dad's.'

'Then he's used to bad driving.'

In fact, she drove the truck well, at high speed like her father, though less oblivious of danger. Steve, with Zac alongside, stole a glance at her gloves, the daft hat. The storm was close and large drops blobbed the windscreen.

'Looks bad,' Di Tuck brooded.

'It's going to pelt, any minute.'

'Not the weather, the *war*.' Her broad lips set tightly.

The cloud-bank was umber and lightning flashed over copses. 'Aye,' wheezed Steve, 'Belgium clobbered, now France on the chop-block.' The sky burst with a bellow. 'The cab leaks,' he reported.

'Always has,' the girl answered, then was silent for a moment. 'Thank your stars you're not Roy, with the Channel behind you.'

'I'd join up,' Steve said quickly. 'I'd go in the Air Force. But then what would your dad do?'

She shrugged, turning up to the farmhouse.

'Come in quick, girl,' Rose shouted. 'Steve, the boss wants the lorry. He's round in the buildings.' Zac stayed with the women. The dog did not relish thunder – besides, Di Tuck intrigued him. Rain engulfed the reunion. It made curtains on windows and dimmed the farm parlour.

Rose said, 'Tuck should be in soon. You know what the man is – doesn't stop till he has to. You're looking well, Dinah; you've gained weight since Christmas.'

Zac napped while they chatted, keeping an ear to their voices. His eyes blinked at the lightning, their white margins showing, for the storm recalled guns and in repose he was wary.

'Have your heard?' Di was asking.

'Not for two or three weeks now.' The tone had grown anxious. 'But Roy's not a writer and his unit keeps moving.'

'Retreating.'

'Withdrawing, they call it, to better positions.'

'The whole army's retreating. If they don't stop damn soon, Ma, they'll be in the Channel. Dear God, what a summer!'

Zac prowled, his ears twitching. The storm had thrown a last tantrum, a clap like a bombshell, before the rain softened and the parlour grew brighter. Rose Tuck became busy. 'I've no time to sit moping – Brindle's calved in the meadow. Someone ought to do something.'

'I'll go.'

'You'll get wet.'

'It's almost stopped raining.'

'Change your clothes, then, and put on some gumboots.'

The dog approved the girl's farm gear. It meant to Zac she belonged, a notion Steve shared soon after, when Di reached the stable. She had the hips to wear trousers. 'Brindle's calved,' she said brusquely. 'I'm taking a cart down.'

'*You* can't fetch her.'

Di humped tack to the cart mare. It was done in a moment: girth strapped, breeching hung, the hames clamped to the collar and the bridle buckled. Steve could not have done better. She led the mare from the stable. 'Brindle's touchy,' he warned her. 'When she's calved she gets stroppy.'

'Steve, you're starting to irk me.' She backed the horse into the cart. 'I was born here. I can manage a cow, Steve.'

She climbed aboard, flipped the reins and left the young man protesting. The sun was back and the fields sweated; there was a clammy warmth in the lane where hogweed and vetch splurged. The old black-maned mare plodded and Di swayed as the cart lurched. From the boards of her chariot she could see, above the hedges, a broad folded landscape turned blue by the heat-haze.

It was a scene the girl treasured. She could not visualize armies, or tanks grinding those acres, or Roy not returning.

At the gate, she got down and stepped into the meadow. Kingcups grew there, and reedy marsh grasses. Brindle was standing by her calf. It lay where she had dropped it, still partly silvered by membrane.

'Come on, Brindle, we'll get you both to a roof and some comfortable bedding.' Di went forward with caution. The cow's head was held low, her eyes watchful. 'I'll not harm your baby.'

Brindle stamped, her horns swinging.

'Cut that out,' Di said tersely. 'You remember me, Brindle.' She stood still and the beast licked the calf. But when the girl ventured closer, the animal grunted and forayed, points levelled.

'Brute!' Di Tuck scrambled backwards. 'You old brute,'

she said, seething. They stood glowering at each other while the calf tried to rise. It jacked its rump off the turf then fell over, its legs still feeble.

Brindle nudged the weak creature but her eye remained sharp, and again Di was routed before she heard Tuck's great laugh booming and caught sight of her father with Zac at the field gate. 'She's beat you,' Tuck bellowed.

'It's not funny.'

'Go on, Zac,' Tuck commanded. 'Draw the old girl away, dog.' The dog skirted the cow, running wide when she charged him. The man strode to the calf. By the time Brindle turned, he had snatched up her newborn and placed it gently in the cart. 'A heifer, Di.' He rubbed the still womb-damp coat. 'Climb up, let's be moving.'

They drove back along the lane. Zac was riding beside them, Brindle's nose at the tailboard as she followed her offspring. From time to time, she called softly or plucked grass from the verges, then caught up with a trot.

'Damned old cow,' Di reflected.

'A good mother; she'd have stuck you for two pins.'

'And you'd have laughed!'

Tuck chuckled. He said, 'You're not looking bad, girl – not for a damned city dweller.'

The dog crossed the rickyard. Rose was washing; Tuck had gone in the Morris to Ringwood market. Steve and Di were around but their work bored the mongrel – they were moving bran from a wagon to the tin-sided building, elevated on stone staddles, which served as a grain store.

Both were white from the meal, powder sticking to their hot faces. Steve humped the sacks to the platform, where Di, with a trolley, wheeled them into the building. 'It wasn't cussedness,' Steve said, his Pierrot's mask anxious, 'I was scared what might happen.'

'You were right.' The girl shunted the trolley gracefully. His solicitude pleased her.

Steve thumped his cap roughly and Zac's responsive nose wrinkled. Through the cloud of fine meal, Steve said, 'Wrong to take chances, a riled cow can be nasty. Keeps her eyes on the target, not like a bull – and she's quicker.'

'The female of the species ...'

'Aye,' mused Steve, twelve stone raised on his shoulder. 'You're doing well,' he informed her, the bag handled deftly. 'When d'you reckon on leaving to get back to that office?'

'Don't know.' She watched his candid face brighten. 'The way things are going, who can tell what might happen? It sounds grim, Steve. The wireless ...'

'Yes.' He climbed up beside her. 'Well, let's see how you've managed.'

The dog moved round the building. At the rear there was clover, and a vixen, sunning herself, looked up as he charged. For a furlong, she ambled, knowing she could outpace him. Then, ears couched, she sprinted. Zac's interest diminished. Now, close to Tuck's covert, he paused and looked back.

Great trees billowed and the farm stood among them, deep-rooted as the elms, as the set of a badger.

Rose was hanging out clothes, her thickly freckled arms lifted. Zac pushed into the wood. It was cool, rank with nettles, and he prowled to its end before reaching the lane where the ponies had galloped. Tail flicking, he stepped out with a quick and determined gait.

At the heath, the dog rested. Scrubby birches and heather stretched away towards forest. Zac lay still as insects swarmed in the sunlight. By the road, a drab cluster of sandbags protected a gun. An army truck pulled up sharply.

'Where's this, soldier?'

'Back of nowhere.'

Zac saw men in strange helmets. They sat hunched in the three-tonner.

'Got a truckload of Frenchmen.'

'How did that lot get over?'

'They hi-jacked a trawler. Some of our lads have made it but there's thousands still waiting. The French beaches are littered. Sending paddleboats for them.'

'Where you heading?'

There was a short-lived discussion then the vehicle departed.

The dog loped forward. The troops meant little to Zac. It was the Wilsons who drew him, their huts near the timbers. He could see the rough ponies, and smoke coming from the dwellings. Keeping low, he pushed on through the heather until, reaching a hollow, he could spy from its lip. The ponies were tethered. A few chickens were scratching with a lean, gaudy cockerel.

He waited. The mean shacks repelled and yet, somehow, engaged him. A child loitered morosely. The dog wriggled closer. The huts were a landmark. He had come to them first on his flight from the forest, from the timber-flanked morass, the shrouding mist.

Now, he froze as the child began screaming.

A woman's high-pitced voice hollered, 'It's the dog; it's the bog cur!'

He turned, tail drooping. A man came from the camp and stones flew at the mongrel. Zac remembered the tinker; he had felt his boot in the hedge the night the tractor was siphoned. The dog ran. He ran like the vixen, neck and tail horizontal, slowing down out of range to glance back, his dark eyes burning. A grey Bofors snout swivelled.

He retraced his path slowly, going down through the pastures, where lambs bleated. The farm was quiet, just the generator throbbing for the day's second milking. In that lull before dusk, the lane became shady and sour with thin cow-muck. The rich grass scoured the cattle. The dog could hear Tuck cursing as he wrestled a bolt with an ill-fitting spanner.

'Blamed stacker ...'

Tuck was wearing his best breeches. The farm implement shuddered. Wilf Tuck was no mechanic. 'Bitch,' he howled, skinning his hands on the stacker. 'I need Steve.'

He stomped indoors, knuckles bleeding. Flies swarmed in the kitchen. Zac slipped under the table, while Tuck batted the insects. 'Where's Steve? Has he been with the milk yet? I need Steve ...'

Rose and Di hugged the wireless. 'It's the news, Tuck – Dunkirk.'

'Damn the news.'

'Roy's across there.'

'The bloody war.'

'I'm worried,' Rose muttered.

'Roy ought never to have gone. He should have stayed on the farm.'

Di said, 'Farm – all you think of!'

'Maybe, girl . . .' The hay stacker was broken, with his grass due for mowing. He had to find hands for the potatoes. There was a horse sick with colic, and he had the copse to pollard, as well as drains to dig in the bottoms. 'Aye,' Tuck told her tiredly, 'so would you, in my breeches. Beasts don't heed the damned wireless. Beasts need milking and feeding, to hell with the news. Weeds need hoeing; potatoes lifting. Someone's got to cope with them.'

He shrugged his broad shoulders. 'Unless the country's to starve.'

Di sat down at the table. Zac put his head in her lap. She said eventually, 'I can hoe and lift earlies . . .'

'You'll be back to town shortly.'

The girl fondled the mongrel.

'What do *you* think?' she murmured. 'What's the rate for the work, Dad? I'd say, if Zac could stay, I can.'

5

When Tuck next went to market, he took the dog. They passed pigs in car-trailers, calves in traps pulled by ponies, cattle wagons. Zac stuck his head from the Morris. He sniffed excitedly. It was new to the mongrel: the old town beneath the cloud hills, built close for street fighting – full of men and beasts out of forests whose depths rang with echoes of ancient wars.

Farmers came here on Wednesdays from Fordingbridge, Wimborne and Cranborne Chase – men from east of the Avon and south of Salisbury. They came from small, forgotten hamlets, dens where scarecrows kept vigil in the great weald's dark remnants. Many of them knew Tuck.

'Any news of the boy, Wilf? They're getting back now, they reckon.'

'He'll take care of himself, Ted.'

'Aye, you'll hear. The lad's smart.'

Roy, they said, was a Tuck and the Tucks were survivors, folk who gave in to nothing. 'Few heifers for sale, Tuck; not your stamp though, I reckon.'

'Don't know as I'm buying.'

He strode with Zac past the pig pens. Other pens held the sheep, Hampshire Downs and some cross-breeds. Dealers mingled with farmers, their eyes mean, their chat pithy. Against the rasp of their comment, the ewes and lambs sounded gentle, refined in their bleating.

Tuck stopped at the cattle. Most were typical foresters, Guernsey crosses; a couple were shorthorns. He held on for the auction. Restive, Zac went exploring.

'Hop it,' somebody told him. The man was loading a wagon, driving steers aboard roughly. His neck was thick; a stout belt strapped his beer-gut. As his stick fell, Zac scooted, falling in with some children.

25

'Run,' they urged, 'or he'll bash you!'

Zac followed the youngsters. Out of school for the lunch break, they romped round the pens, stroking sheep, kicking pebbles. Some had sweets and he sniffed them. 'Hey!' They snatched their bags from him. 'Don't you know sweets are rationed?'

Someone gave him a sherbert. They laughed as he puckered; then, fondling the mongrel, they scampered on, shouting. Gas masks swung from their shoulders.

Zac ran with them.

At the steps in the square, a man was selling horse collars. Zac paused, interested. 'Come on,' called the children and once more he bounded, now past shop-fronts and street stalls. He saw new prongs for hay forks and bundles of bean-sticks. There were chickens in cages and a woman sold duck eggs. Geese cackled and day-old chicks cheeped in boxes.

The dog threaded the stacked pavements. The curbs were piled with field produce. There were samples from gardens: peas, shallots and asparagus.

'Go on, kids,' a voice bellowed. 'Back to school and don't dawdle.'

A white line crawled above them. People tipped their heads backwards. Peering up between chimneys, old men squinted fiercely. The thin vapour-trail idled. 'One of ours,' they decided. 'There's been no raid warning.'

Zac stopped at the schoolyard.

'What's his name?' asked the teacher.

'Zac – it's there on his collar.'

'Well, he can't come inside. He must wait until class ends.'

But Zac did not linger. Alone, the dog thought of Tuck and the green-painted farm truck. Doubling back on his scent, he moved again through the vendors with their brooms, ropes and produce, passed the shadows of tap-rooms and looked for the livestock. The auction was over.

A man was hosing the standings. Zac watched, ruminating. He had left Tuck at the ring. Now, the compound was empty. All he smelled was pipe-dottle and squashed cigarette-ends. He went back to the wagons. Hooves were rattling on ramps and he heard cattle lowing.

One distraught beast was roaring – a cow had slipped to her knees. Zac drew closer. Weaving through the fraught creatures, he saw the pot-bellied drover's bludgeon flailing.

'Cut that out,' a voice ordered.

Zac's ears pricked at the inflection; the growl was familiar. 'B'God, man, what *are* you?' A great fist was thrust forward. It snatched the stick and destroyed it, then Tuck flung the parts from him. 'Don't ever do that while *I'm* here. Next time, mister, I'll thump you.'

Tuck was gentle with cattle. He respected their natures and would speak softly to them, by name if he owned them. He turned his back on the drover.

Zac was crouching. He watched the drover start forward. The man lunged at the farmer, but Zac's yelp was a warning and Tuck came round with a fist cocked. The dog flinched at the jolting impact. Stunned, the drover lurched backwards. He seemed suddenly spineless, pitching over the pen rails to sprawl amidst pig dung.

Tuck considered the mongrel. 'You're a fine one, you beggar.' He rubbed his knuckles, his chest heaving. 'Thought you'd run off and left us. It's late, let's be going.'

He drove home at full throttle.

Zac sat close to the farmer. Blood oozed on Tuck's fist, its scent strong to the mongrel. The lanes were hot, the tarmac melted. It was a week since it had rained – and a day before Zac fought the shepherd's dog.

They shaped up on the waste ground. So far, Zac had been patient. Now he challenged the sheepdog. The big grey animal bristled. His partner was working and he had come for the mongrel through the wiry-stemmed mayweed, his heart set on mischief.

Zac surprised him. There was a heap of road-gravel piled high near the farm track. Here, the mongrel had hidden, stepping out at the last moment. Thistle-bounded, it was a place made for a fight, if for little else.

Tuck's mongrel looked ugly. The friendly face was

27

distorted, folded back from the snout to expose fangs and molars. His coat stared. The stray seemed big now and savage. But not as big as the sheepdog, whose wolfish mouth chattered.

Flank to flank, the dogs circled. They stepped with strangely stiff movements, legs rigid, tails lofted, a low roaring inside them which grew louder in spasms. At that moment of tension, they seemed swollen with battle, all life dwarfed around them.

Next instant, Zac was sprawling on his back, the sheepdog above him, boring down at his throat. Their jaws clashed. It was explosively sudden. Then, with dust-raising fury, the conflict resounded.

Rose and Di looked up quickly. They were cleaning the hen huts, scrubbing dung-boards and slats and creosoting the woodwork where red mites had harboured. The stain and stench were tenacious. The two had worked quietly. Once, Rose Tuck had ventured, 'He's keen on you, Dinah. Don't tease him.'

'Come on, Ma, he's not simple.'

'Nor one of your town lads. Don't you lead him along, Di. Steve takes things to heart.'

'Saints alive, I won't eat him!' Then, a few seconds later, 'What's that?' she said, startled. 'Sounds like Zac being murdered.'

'He's fighting!'

Rose snatched a broom and they ran through the orchard, drawn by the commotion. It grew louder. The snarling dogs raised a dust storm. Spinning, they flattened the grasses and rolled among thistles, then struck the pile of dumped gravel. It avalanched pebbles and deluged the animals. Then they were whirling like demons, their coats torn and bleeding.

Zac fought stubbornly. Not only was he the smaller but also the elder of the dogs, and his wind was shorter. Jaws crackling, he tussled, as his antagonist rounded, and again their fangs rattled.

'Don't get near,' Tuck's wife shouted. 'Don't touch them, they're crazy!'

She plied the broom at full length. It was like stirring a wasps' nest, increasing the turmoil. Now, Zac was on top, at the throat of the sheepdog.

'*Zac!*' bawled Di.

There was a pail by the yard trough and she soused them with water. At last, the larger dog broke, sloping off down the track while the mongrel watched, bristling. 'You thug,' Di reproved him.

Zac flicked his tail feebly. His ears were raddled, his neck mauled. She washed the blood from him roughly. 'Let him be,' Rose admonished, 'he doesn't deserve it.'

But her daughter's eyes twinkled. 'Come here, you old brawler.' She cleaned up the lesions. 'I suppose you've proved something. You don't give in, you and Tuck. You're a pair of damned donkeys.' The dog shook and looked smug. He was content with the outcome.

Wilf Tuck chuckled. 'Old Shep's dog? Shep'll moan to high heaven.'

'It's not crippled,' the girl said. They watched Zac lick a foreleg.

'I'll be damned,' Tuck reflected. 'Little Zac and that wolf! Shep'll cuss like a trooper – he gave ten bob for that herder.'

'It's a good worker,' Rose said.

'So's Zac – and cost nothing!'

Tuck went back to work cackling and the dog nursed his fight wounds. He wore an air of importance. As the day closed, he returned to the farm track, stalking up to the road-stones. Once more, Zac walked stiffly. For a while, he bristled, scent-marking and strutting. The spoor of conflict was heady, as strong on the air as his mongrel pride.

A star glimmered.

Zac paused, eyeing the orchard. The shapes that evening were curious. The trees were crowded with chickens, which formed dark blobs on the branches. The dog barked, his snout wrinkling. The birds should be in their houses, safe by dusk from the vixen. Instead they were roosting like pheasants.

29

He barked again, for attention. In the gloom, he heard voices.

'They're all over the orchard – Ma's damned Leghorn pullets!'

'Clean huts – you've upset them.'

A torch swept the trees.

'Steve, for God's sake, the black-out!'

'Can't be helped – have to catch them. Wild as pigeons, Leghorns are.'

'There's five score up there somewhere. I'll fetch Tuck.'

'No, we'll manage.' Steve was climbing the first tree. 'Find some sacks; I'll start catching.'

Zac raced Di to the barn. With sacks and twine, the girl returned to the orchard. Steve leaned out of the apple tree. He had three birds by the legs, their heads dangling. Di bagged them and the young man climbed higher.

'Careful, Steve,' the girl warned him.

Zac pounced. A bird had crouched on the ground and the dog held it captive until Di took it from him. Steve swung down with more pullets. It was a slow, risky process. Once, a dead bough snapped loudly and he clung to the tree-trunk, fowls flapping and squawking. Di muttered.

The dusk thickened. Dew had spread and Tuck's shorthorn bull bellowed. 'We've caught most,' Steve called hoarsely. 'The rest are too high.' He came down through the shadows. 'Heads,' he shouted, 'I'm jumping!' His boots thumped and he staggered.

Zac saw Di's arms support him. For a while, the two were close, the girl amused by Steve's confusion, then a shriek pierced the evening.

'*Tuck!*' It came from the farmhouse. The dog started forward. '*Di!*' The others were running. 'It's Roy,' Rose was screaming, 'he's safe back in England. Roy phoned. He's in England ...'

6

Zac considered the soldier. He was tall – tall as Tuck, though leaner – his raw-boned face weary. He wore the rank of lance-corporal, the stripes newly issued. 'Dead men's boots,' he said drily, shrugging off the promotion.

The dog nosed the table. There had been piquant arrangements, smells of cooking and curing and sausage-meat making. Zac smelled brawn for the soldier, cold ham and pig's trotters. But Roy was not eating, just pecking the helpings.

He said, 'I thought food was rationed.'

'Not tonight, son,' Rose told him.

Tuck carved with fierce relish. He was pleased for the women. Rose had raided her garden to brighten the parlour and, like Di, looked her best. The two women were striking, their country skins amber, in floral prints. 'We'll soon have the lad eating.' Tuck thanked God for Roy's safety. 'A few days of farmwork!'

'He's not here to work,' Rose said. 'He's home for a rest, Tuck.'

'To please *himself*,' Di suggested.

Zac's eye held the soldier. Food was left on his plate and the dog ventured closer.

'Aye, to please himself,' Tuck said, his face beaming. 'The lad's where he belongs. A few days' farming will brace him, take his mind from the army. He can help me this evening.'

'He will not,' Rose shot quickly. 'He'll be putting his feet up.'

Roy smiled. It was the ghost of a glimmer. Feeding Zac from his leavings, he said, changing the subject, 'Where'd you get this old dustbin?'

Di said, 'Zac's the farm mystery.' She ragged the tricoloured mongrel. 'You're a puzzlement, aren't you? He's

31

our bearer of luck, don't you see – Zac brought you home to us.'

'He was starving,' said Rose. 'Now look at him!'

'Fighting fit,' Tuck said proudly.

He pushed his plate back and stretched, chest and elbows extending. He seemed, to Zac, to fill the parlour. 'Tell you this, boy, he's useful. I'd not sell him. Put a record on, Di. Let the lad hear some music.' Di crouched on her haunches, the bright skirt spread round her. She cranked the gramophone briskly. It wheezed *Run Rabbit*, Tuck's favourite.

Rose cleared the dishes, with Di helping.

'*Run, run, run,*' the box crackled.

'Run, run run,' boomed the farmer.

The soldier stroked the dog gently, his dark-circled eyes brooding. Outside, bees laboured late, the trees loud with their rumble. The record blipped and Di retrieved it. At last, Tuck declared briefly, 'Well, I've work to get finished – you coming to help, Roy?'

'Get on, damn you,' Rose told him. 'Can't you see the boy's sleeping?' Roy had sprawled in the armchair. 'If you must go, go quietly.'

'Asleep?'

'You and your work!' snarled the woman, but she took his hand, crooning, 'He's safe, Tuck, thank heaven. Just let the boy rest, man.'

'Yes, poor Roy,' Di reflected. 'He'll sleep till the war ends.' Yet he was out the next morning, at work in the hayfield, and she climbed the rick to him. He forked hay to the corners, filling in with broad layers. 'You don't *have* to,' she shouted.

'Nor you, Dinah.'

'War effort. It helps.'

'And there's Steve.'

'*So?*' she bridled.

'Good old Steve,' Roy mused darkly, outlined against the clouds, thigh-deep in the hayrick. The tractor was sweeping, chugging up with great mounds of the sweet sun-bleached grasses while Tuck rode the horse-rake. Perched high between its wheels, the man juddered and sweated, heaving

32

the crude upright lever to lift the tines, dropping trim rows of rakings.

His voice echoed. 'Be sure there's good ventilation. I don't want that rick heating. If it burns, so will you, lad!'

'When *you're* here,' Di told Roy, 'the man's happy.'

'When I'm sweating!'

'He's built the farm for you, Roy.'

'Slaved for the farm, Di. I wouldn't.'

The dog climbed the ladder. It was one of Zac's farm skills. Di was gazing out from the ricktop to where the lanky corn rippled. There was some rust in the wheat, a patch of spot on the oats but, in general, fair prospects. Zac breathed the land's odours. Far off, engines thundered.

They came nearer and Zac flinched.

'Get down, Di!'

The girl lay prone as the roar swelled. Now it blared, reached crescendo. Like a bolt, the grey bomber stormed over, barely clearing the hayrick. The air vibrated. Zac could make out black crosses, the fliers peering through perspex. Fleetingly, the sky darkened, then the Heinkel had passed and the soldier was rising.

The girl hugged the mongrel.

'It's all right,' she said tautly. 'It's all right, Zac, it's gone now.'

Rose Tuck blamed the aircraft. Soon afterwards, Zac vanished, his meal left uneaten. Rose viewed the bowl glumly. She had cursed the dog but she missed him. It was like putting the clock back; as if his stay had been imagined.

'He'll turn up,' Tuck assured here. 'He's maybe down in the village.'

But when Rose phoned the forge, there was no word of the mongrel. Rutter's wife had not seen him, nor had Murton's Doc Benson as he called on his patients. Rose walked to the farmyard. 'Steve,' she yelled, 'is that dog back?'

Steve and Roy looked up slowly. The bull was at the trough, twitching where the flies crawled, its tasselled tail swishing. To Rose, the bull was a monster. Its red and cream

33

flank was muck-soiled, and when it pawed, the dust billowed.

'Not yet. He'll be back, though.'

Steve was holding the nose-lead; Roy, a rope to the bull's horns. Rose recoiled from the creature, whose lips dribbled water. Its small round eyes swivelled. They were glazed, enigmatic. Tuck's wife kept her distance.

Roy said, perched on the trough's end, 'Reckon Zac's gone off courting. Don't fret, Ma, he's love-struck.'

'Not as I know,' Rose told him.

Roy grinned. 'It's the season. Ask Steve here, *he'll* tell you.'

'Never mind,' snapped the woman. She quizzed Steve, who looked sheepish. 'You watch what you're up to, that animal's dangerous.'

The bull flared its nostrils. Dotted with moisture, the ringed nose sniffed the buildings, its snorted breath pungent. A broad hoof scraped the ground. For a while, they were dust-blurred – the men, the bull and the bull-pen – then the gritty cloud settled and Steve said, composed now, 'The bull's shut up too often. He'd be better out grazing.'

Better sold, Rose considered, but you could not have told Tuck that. 'Damn the dog, Steve, where is he?'

'I'll take a look when work's over.' Steve gazed at the water. Tuck's bull had stopped drinking. 'Di – Miss Di – said she'd help me.'

'Count me out,' said the soldier. 'Three's a crowd.' The grin widened.

Steve turned the bull sharply.

'Bring him in,' he urged, frowning, 'he's drunk all he wants. Mind him, Roy, he gets stroppy.' The beast swung its quarters. With the fleshy neck bending, the bull shimmied sideways, tail raised, its feet dancing. The men forced it forward. By the time they had penned it, Rose was back indoors, breathless.

'That you, Tuck?' He was scrubbing his fingers under the kitchen tap. 'He'll kill someone,' she blurted; 'that damned bull will kill someone.'

'He's all right, girl – just needs talking to firmly.'

'The cowman won't lead him.'

'Man's too old for the job, Rose.'

'Well, it's on your head, Wilf. Don't say I've not warned you.'

Tuck dried his hands, grunting.

Rose said, 'Zac's not returned yet.'

'Stop worrying, woman.' Yet Tuck was as anxious. He had just passed the buildings and seen a rat scuttle. It had come from a culvert and crossed to the stables. The dog would have caught it. As a ratter, Zac was lethal. The man missed the mongrel. 'He knows the way back home,' Tuck said.

'But will he *try* to come back, Tuck? That plane scared him. The dog's frightened of aircraft.' Rose eyed the door bleakly. Zac had strayed from one home; he could stray from another. She pulled on an apron. 'Blasted mongrel,' she muttered, 'I don't want him to leave us; I've got fond of the beggar.'

'He'll return when he's hungry.' Tuck tugged his cap briskly.

'It's gone his mealtime,' his wife said.

'I'm going to look at the earlies then I'll drop by the warren. He could be digging for rabbits.'

'Hope to God he's not buried.'

'He'll be safe.' Tuck strode up to the potatoes. In a while, his son joined him. Roy carried the shotgun, his eye on the hedges. It was like the old evenings, before the war started. The sun was warm, though now dipping, and mallard flew over.

The sound of doves came from woodlands, full and slow in the stillness. Tuck paused, hands in pockets. For one brief summer moment, the cares of work lifted and he relaxed with the soldier. Neither spoke. The smell of earth pleased the farmer. So did Roy – tall, well-muscled.

It had not all been pointless: the years of toil, loss and heartaches. Tuck viewed the long-shadowed acres. It was good land, Roy's future. Peace would crown the farm's prospects.

He broke the silence by saying, 'I'll sit back when it's over.

When the war's done, you'll run things.'

Roy averted his features. 'First, we've got to hold out, Dad.'

'Bah!' said Tuck, bloody-minded.

'They could invade any moment.'

The farmer looked scornful. Tuck trusted in history – nine centuries unconquered – to defy the logistics. 'Tell you what,' he said roughly, 'the war's done something for farming. It's gained us due recognition. They've discovered we matter.'

He snatched a handful of soil. It was warm, moistly textured. That was the nation's assurance when blockade closed the sea-lanes. He let it run through his fingers. 'You'll have a living to turn to,' Tuck averred, 'when it's over. There'll be no more depressions.'

'No?' said Roy, his mind drifting. The soldier pondered his squad-mates, some dead, some still missing. There was a new group recruiting, called a commando. He had thought of applying. 'Listen, Dad, a dog's barking.'

'One of Shep's dogs,' Tuck told him.

'Ma's upset.'

'She's got used to the mongrel. Damned if we want him to leave, Roy, he's as good as a farmhand. But I reckon we'll find him. Most likely, he's hunting.'

'Got a nose for a scut?'

'He'd find a gnat in a covert!'

Tuck scooped earth from the potatoes. Easing a clump of stalks upwards, he exposed the pale tubers. 'A few more days,' he said, straightening. 'Give them a week, they'll be ready. Should make five tons an acre.'

'I'll be back at camp,' Roy said.

'Aye,' growled Tuck, thinking: just when a strong arm was needed. But the farmer kept quiet. Roy took aim at a rabbit and let it bolt without firing. Wilf Tuck watched, disbelieving, then shrugged. 'Let's look in the warren.'

The sun had turned crimson.

As the evening shades deepened, the wild roses folded, their tangled bines viprous. The straight potato stems purpled. Tuck and son trod the headland, making tracks for

36

the coombe where the rabbits were thickest. In that old neglected corner, briar and bramble grew densely and burrows abounded.

The men stepped over wire fencing. A brake of hawthorn shelved down and the path dropped abruptly to close-nibbled grass strewn with dry rabbit buttons.

Roy Tuck eyed his father. There was no sound of the dog there. It seemed oddly deserted. Most warm summer evenings, the coombe swarmed with rabbits. Now all that stirred were the insects. They formed small noiseless squadrons where the last rays of sun fell.

Tuck said, 'Something's been this way.'

A twig cracked.

'Hear?' the younger man whispered. 'Over there, by the gorse.'

They approached the bush softly. The air was herb-scented and the high clouds had reddened. Roy listened. Pushing on by the gorse, he almost ran into Di. She was standing with Steve, the girl and farmhand embracing. So lost were they in kissing, they had not heard the others. Glimpsing Tuck, Roy was thankful the gun was in his hands.

7

The dog stole round the hutment. This time, he remained hidden, a wraith in the heather. Once, a pony stopped browsing and raised its head quickly, but the mongrel had frozen and the cobby mare resumed grazing. Again, Zac slithered forward.

A child was bawling. The sound came from the dwellings, and with it, more plaintive, a woman's deep sobbing. Then a man's voice said harshly, 'That'll do you no good, Sal. It won't bring our Tom back.' The rough tone was familiar: the rasp of the Wilsons.

The dog reached the forest. He looked back at the ponies. The heath seemed suddenly brilliant, the timbers forbidding, but Zac did not linger. The crude trail was rutted and he put his nose to it.

The smell was of tractors. Felled trees had been dragged, tearing, crushing the ground-growth, and he followed the score marks. A scabrous chatter alarmed him as magpies flapped through the shadows, their scolding abrasive. Stabbed by splinters of sunlight, they became iridescent. Then, as Zac went in deeper, the forest grew lonesome.

He stopped and lifted a forepaw. He put it down, then raised the other.

Ivy trailed from a tree-stump. Where it grew at a tangent, creeping over the path, a coiled serpent was sleeping. Zac drew back from the adder.

As he marched, the gloom thickened. A rhythmic thudding resounded, then the crash of tall timber. At last, the lumber track widened and the dog reached a clearing, where two woodsmen were working and a fire burned the off-cuts. Like most men on the land now, the couple were grizzled. They toiled with skilled, sparing movements.

Zac watched from a thicket. There was a greyness of light

hanging over the tree-butts, which came from the fire-smoke. The dog did not like it. In his sleep, he still twitched when the grey nightmare haunted him. Yet he sought the path forward.

The men trimmed the next timber. Cutting back the root-buttress, they hacked out a gullet, their axes ringing. Zac saw the raw, white-fleshed throat, then a saw screeched. Two-handed, they plied it, working in from the far side, above the plane of the axe blows.

They paused briefly. One of the men drove in wedges, then the big saw cut deeper.

'She'll do.' They stepped backwards.

Zac saw the tree's crown above him. It was flailing the sky-dome, its great branches creaking, towering over the mongrel. As he watched, the tree tottered, its massive trunk slanting. Limbs caught and clutched neighbours, but they had no power to hold it. Twigs and boughs snapped; leaves trembled.

'Flaming hell, there's a dog!'

'You're right. What's he doing?'

Zac was getting out quickly, scratched by brush as he retreated. Above, the falling tree moaned, its descent growing steeper, its arms flung widely. Then the first branches started to smash as they came down around him. Zac ran on through the debris. 'It's missed him,' said one man.

The prostrate timber shuddered.

'Luck o' the devil,' his mate said.

'That'll teach him to wander. Clear off, you thick beggar – there's more bones in those bogs than a haddock's back!'

'I'm not a schoolgirl,' Di shouted.

'You ought to know better.' Tuck's anger resounded. Rose stomped from the farmhouse, fetched out by the voices. Di could fight like a cat when she and Tuck started. The two had paused in the lane, Steve stationed between them. Rose feared for his chances.

'Dad, it's none of your business.'

'*My* farmhand?' Tuck thundered.

'God Almighty.' Rose stopped them. 'I could hear you

indoors!' In the dusk-laden silence, a gunshot exploded, the muffled sound rolling. Roy, she guessed, on the headlands. She looked from Tuck to the young woman. 'They could hear you in Murton. Lord's sake, what's got in you?'

'It's my fault,' Steve said gravely.

'Is it hell,' Di corrected. 'You keep out of it, Steven.'

'Well?' Tuck's wife prompted sharply.

Tuck said, 'Woman, I caught them.' His big face was ferocious, doubly dark in the gloaming. 'They were down in the warren.'

Di said, '*Caught*!' with derision.

Rose looked hard at her daughter. She had warned Di to be careful but, like Tuck, she was headstrong. Di had always ridden roughshod. She would leave Steve upended.

'Aye,' said Tuck, 'caught it was, girl.'

Di whirled, her eyes fiery. 'I don't care what you call it, it's 1940,' she shouted. 'I'll do what I fancy. We *do*, now – if you'd noticed. I'll kiss someone else next time!'

Rose could see Steve's mind struggling. Di would leave the men plodding, more alike than they reckoned. But Tuck was used to his daughter and their clashes harmed neither. It was Steve who was tender. He said slowly, his face troubled, 'What I'd call it was courting.' Rose suppressed the groan in her. 'If she'd have me, I'd wed her.'

The stillness was eerie. It was a strangely hushed moment – so Rose would muse later – the four in the twilight as the first bats adventured and the land darkened. They might have been Druids, that small black-etched group, until Wilf Tuck said, 'Wed? Wed my daughter? You're daft, lad.'

'That'll do,' Rose rebuked him. 'Steve's a good boy; you know it. Of course Dinah likes him. But she's got other friends, Steve.'

'Them in London?'

Tuck said, 'Don't waste your time, lad.'

Rose said, 'Let him be, Wilf. Get on home, Steve,' she added. 'We're all tired and hungry. Here comes Roy – he'll want supper.'

The fifth figure loomed darkly, drawing out of the evening.

40

The rest could just see the soldier before they lost him in gloom where a rick screened the eve star. He showed again at the yard gate. 'Hey,' called Roy, 'look who I've found!'

Zac appeared, his tail swinging.

The mongrel was weary, his tongue drooped and he limped, but he greeted them warmly. With relief, they responded. Tuck crowed. 'There – I told you,' he beamed. 'He's back safely.' Steve eyed the dog, grinning.

'He's full of thorns,' Di cried, anguished. 'Come on, Dad, help us pull them.'

Zac enjoyed the attention.

The bats were zig-zagging, hawking over the stables, and one of Tuck's horses whinnied. Rose inhaled the night odours, catching scent of honeysuckle and elder from the hedges. 'Dear Lord,' she thought, close-lipped, 'all it took was a mongrel!' The fools were clucking like chickens.

She fed the dog fondly.

Roy had left by the next Monday. Tuck was digging potatoes and Steve was driving the tractor, turning up the smooth tubers while the labour gang sweated in the scorching July sun. Most of the pickers were women, sturdy, weathered, some with men in the forces and all used to field work. Murton offered none other. They brought toddlers who squabbled.

Zac allowed them to scrag him.

'Mind that dog,' snapped the women. 'You touch him, he'll bite you.'

'That he'll not!' Di corrected. She was missing her brother, brooding on his departure. At least Roy was in Blighty, she thought, her humour tetchy. She stooped and set the pace fiercely. Now and then a back would stretch, a brow be mopped with soiled fingers. Tuck weighed-up on the scales, heaving sacks to the Morris.

Zac settled beside him. The noise of youngsters was strident, but a deeper sound reached the mongrel. It was muffled at first, like bees in a lime tree, a multitudinous chanting on the threshold of his hearing. Only the dog caught

41

the rumble as it grew and became malign; then the others peered upwards, their hot faces fearful.

'Planes,' Di murmured.

'Must be high,' said a woman.

In bloody scores, Tuck was thinking. He could make out wings flashing far up, almost midge-like. The sun dazzled and he lost them. Then another batch glittered. They came on in formations, in great swarms, he thought, gawping.

'Get the kids in the ditches!'

He was no longer loading. With Di, Tuck was running, catching hold of the infants, steering them to the hedges. 'Keep down,' he commanded.

Zac had joined the dispersal, outpacing the women. A toddler was bawling. The small boy had tripped over and Zac stopped beside him and licked the child's face. The drone deafened. They sat, the two, amid tubers, the youngster clutching the farm dog.

'Over here,' Di was screaming. 'Come on, Zac, bring him over.'

Zac grabbed the child's clothes. Gently, he tugged the boy forward as hands reached out, helping.

Tuck looked up to see fighters. The trails of vapour made circles as the silver specks wheeled and twisted. Like minnows, they darted, so high they were noiseless until one became larger, its revved engine screaming, its nose down. A Spitfire.

'Pull out,' breathed the farmer. Then, as the screaming grew louder, 'Bale out of it, damn you.' But no parachute opened. The plane went down beyond the heath, headlong into the forest, the scream aborted. There was a hush, then the *crump*. Nothing more – except the smudge of black fumes.

'Poor beggar,' Tuck grunted. The lad would never be found; they would not search the morass.

'They're passing over,' Di muttered.

'Somebody will cop it.' Tuck chalked a stroke on the truck, back at work, keeping tally.

The girl fondled the mongrel. The contact was soothing. She said, 'Two of theirs bought it.'

42

'Bloody waste,' he said grimly. 'Wasted lives. Bloody madness.'

He thought of Roy on the headland.

Again, the women were bending, earth clogging their fingers. And now the children were pleased, finding spent bullet cases the warplanes had scattered. Steve climbed back on the tractor. 'At least *they're* happy,' he mumbled.

'For the moment,' Di told him. 'It's begun now in earnest. There'll be no end to it, will there? God knows what'll happen.'

I know one thing,' he answered. I'm not staying much longer – not while others are dying. I'm not tied to this tractor.'

'That's up to you,' Di said.

'Unless – I'd do what *you* wanted.'

'Christ,' she said, her hair tossing, 'make your own bloody mind up, I'm not in charge of you!'

8

Dust and chaff filled the rickyard, assailing the nostrils,
exercising the tear ducts. A brown cloud wreathed the
thresher. It begrimed hair and clothing, clogged boots and
made necks raw. The contractor's team toiled in silence,
inured to the debris.

Three men worked on the stack, tossing sheaves to the
deck, where a fourth cut the bonds and a fifth fed the drum,
his face goggled and dirt-lined. Others hauled away corn
sacks, pitched and stacked disgorged straw and – least envied
among them – cleaned under the engine, raking chaff, dust
and cavings.

The pounding monster vibrated. Strap-driven from a
Fordson, the thresher shook with such violence the men on
top shuddered. Tuck bagged-up a grain sample. It was the
first threshed since harvest, a quick sale to pay bills and make
straw for the winter.

'Looks fair,' said the contractor.

'It'll do,' Tuck accepted. The corn was clean. There was,
perhaps, a ton an acre. He peered through the dust, wiping
his lips with his knuckles. 'More'n *he* will,' he shouted. 'Him
on top – that's a Wilson.'

'What say?' bawled the other. The din drowned their
voices. The contractor swung a sledge, checking the wheels
on the engine, ramming home wooden chocks.

'Him cutting bonds – he's a tinker.'

'Aye,' affirmed the contractor, 'one of them from the
hutment.'

'A thieving Wilson,' Tuck grumbled.

'Mister, men are men these days. You're lucky to get them.
He's a good enough worker.'

'Wilsons!' muttered the farmer.

The old yard cat slipped past them, worn fangs at the

ready. The first mice were appearing, scuttling out of the stack as the thresher reduced it. Chickens chased them, their wings flapping. The rats would go to the bottom and lie low to the end, when the last sheaves were lifted. Then the dog would be needed.

The contractor was saying, 'They found these parachutes buried ...'

'What parachutes?' Tuck said.

The other leered, his eyes shining. He was a small man, legs bandy. 'We've to watch out for strangers; report our suspicions.'

Tuck spat, swinging a corn sack. It looked light in his fists – a hundredweight and a half. He said, 'To hell with suspicions; I've got more than suspicions. I've caught them draining my tractor. I've had ponies on my crops. Never mind your damned strangers, it's the Wilsons need watching.'

He ran hen-wire round the stack, planting sticks to support it. When the rats at length bolted, the wire would contain them. 'Parachutes?' he said, pausing.

'Out the west side o' Murton.'

'Blamed war ...'

'Fifth Column, they reckon, dropped to stir up confusion.'

'Huh!' the farmer responded.

'First stage of invasion.'

'Nought but talk,' Tuck disparaged. 'They've had the whole of the summer; they won't cross in the winter.'

'There's still time,' said the contractor.

The farmer took up a pitchfork. He shrugged, calling the dog, and Zac jumped the wire as the last sheaves were lifted. 'Seek the beggars,' Tuck told him, forking over the faggots on which the rick had been founded. The smaller man stopped the tractor and the thresher's roar dwindled. Its final gasp expired corn husks. 'Seek 'em, Zac, they'll be there.'

Other men joined them, prodding.

The first rat reached the wire and Zac's teeth tossed it deftly. It lay still, its neck broken. Tuck transfixed a brown monster. Rats plagued the farm buildings. Every door had been gnawed, almost every sack ravaged. He showed no mercy. A scaley tail swished and vanished.

Zac rummaged the sticks then leaped up, his head shaking. A big sow rat had caught him, biting into an ear, where the creature hung grimly. Tuck raised his fork but held back. Enraged, Zac put his head down and scraped off the rodent. As the rat ran, he killed it.

From the top of the thresher, the begrimed bond-cutter watched, slowly closing the clasp-knife. 'No-good dog,' the man brooded.

'Is that so?' scoffed the feed-man. He grinned, raising his goggles.

'The devil's cur,' said the tinker.

'Got the size of you, has he?'

Tuck had turned the last sticks. There were no more rats in them. Six lay dead. Mice were fleeing, boring into the chaff, striking out across puddles. The dog sought the yard trough, then, his thirst appeased, departed. Fresh scents beckoned. A leaf planed as he went, and more fell, tumbling. In the fierce autumn dazzle, he could hear finches calling and the wing-sounds of insects.

Small birds mobbed in hedges, ganging up for the winter. They flew ahead of the mongrel, pitching into the warren, bursting out, batting forward. Zac stopped. Someone was standing in the hollow. The dog could make out a topcoat, a pale face, the eyes staring, but nothing moved and the stranger was silent.

For a moment, Zac waited. The other's stillness bemused and disconcerted the dog, who withdrew, his spine tingling, as if from a spectre. The form did not shift. It remained in the coombe, an eerie shape in the shadows.

When Zac reached the sheep fold, Shep's bitch was alone. Her companion was working and the young female was restless. Bored, she welcomed Zac warmly. Rumps jigging, they flirted. Forgetting the stranger, Zac romped like a pup until the shepherd's voice stopped them.

'It's you, you mad beggar!' The shuffling Shep hobbled nearer. 'Get you gone from that bitch!'

Zac sloped back to the bushes. In the lane, wheels were

moving, heavy implements crunching. They were shifting the thresher. The dog returned to the hollow. Alert now, he stepped lightly, mindful of his encounter with the coombe's silent figure.

October's haze drifted. It formed dank strands, like sheep's wool caught on fencing, thickening in the depression. Zac sniffed the vapour. For a while, he looked round but the place was deserted – except for the linnets, which passed through, chattering.

Di drove up to the station. She touched Steve's arm then, 'Good luck,' she said quickly, both hands back on the wheel. 'Give my love to the smoke.' To poor bomb-blasted London, she thought.

'Wish you were coming.' Steve dithered.

'Get on, man. Got your warrant?' He looked a boy in his good jacket, fresh-scrubbed and his hair cut. The girl feared for his chances. 'You'll be back; they won't eat you. It's only a selection board.'

'Aircrew – they're fussy.'

'Go on, the train's coming. Wait,' she countered, 'stroke the dog. Zac'll bring you good fortune.'

Steve ruffled the mongrel, who beamed, perched between them. 'You won't tell Tuck or your ma?'

'Christ's sake, Steve, I'm not dotty! It's your week off. It's *your* business.'

'Aye.' His gaze lingered on her.

'See you soon,' she said firmly.

'At the farm. I'll be back for beet-carting. Don't worry, I'll . . .'

'Scram, Steve!'

'I'll be back for the carting.'

He hauled his bag from the truck and she watched him to the platform, lost in steam, then a shape in the carriage. She half-wished she had kissed him, but knew her mother had been right: that mistake had been made already.

Zac had taken Steve's cab seat. She gunned the truck from the halt and drove fast towards Ringwood.

Poor Steve! And poor Tuck, the girl mused – that was, if Steve passed the test, which she reckoned uncertain. She could not see Steve with wings; for all his dreams, he was no flier, just a nice earthbound fellow, a bloke with a tractor. And that, she thought, could be Tuck's luck.

'Damn them, Zac,' she said briskly. 'When did *we* have an outing?'

She pulled into the market and strode round the stockpens. Heads turned, farmers mumbled. Zac followed, tail jaunty. 'Miss Tuck?' said a dealer. 'Glad to see you've left London. No place to be these days. So you're home helping Mum?'

'Helping Dad,' she corrected.

'Here to spend the farm profits?'

'No,' she said, 'my slave-wages.' She marched on, hands in pockets. 'Hold it, Zac, look at *that*!' She had stopped at the shops. In a small bow-fronted window, the sheer nightdress was sumptuous. She thought of Steve and laughed abruptly, so the dog looked up at her. 'No good, Zac, I need the coupons.' To dress, she thought, like a farmhand.

The girl glimpsed her reflection. 'Dear God,' she said quietly, depressed by the image: trousered hips, crumpled sweater – Steve's notion of beauty. They would not know her in London. They would be shocked by her hair – supposing *they* were still living and not under the rubble.

'I could use a drink,' Di said. 'Come on, dog, I need bracing.' She ordered ale and a pie, which she fed to the mongrel. The tap-room was crowded, filled mainly with farmers. A pair of soldiers came over, the more venturesome grinning.

'Landgirl?' he asked brashly.

She let them chat, scarcely listening. They fondled Zac and Di thawed slightly. She thought of Roy, newly-stationed in Scotland, maybe looking for friendship. The men beside her were gunners. They spoke of various regiments. 'There's another lot,' Di said, 'just formed – the Commandos.'

They laughed. 'Tarzan's army!'

'Rough lads,' said the quiet one.

'Mad as hatters,' his mate said. 'They cocked up their first outing – went to Guernsey and muffed it. You're better off with *real* soldiers. Who d'you know in the Commandos?'

'My brother's just joined them.'

The soldiers straightened their faces.

'Early days,' said the first. 'They'll shape up.'

She let them talk.

Di drove home in low spirits. The countryside seemed a backwoods cut off from excitement, from friends of her own age. 'Zac, we're lumbered – old men and damned scarecrows!' Even the dog had grey whiskers.

Zac slept in the Morris on the way back. They had picked up some farm goods and the lamp-oil Rose wanted. The stuff shook in the back as the truck groaned and rattled. Di could see shorthorns grazing and hear the westerly howling.

She slowed down, her eyes narrow, as a man came from one of the hen huts straddling the skyline and ran into the woodland. Di could not place the figure but it was too slim to be Tuck's. At all events it had vanished.

9

'Filching eggs,' Tuck concluded.

'A parachutist, d'you reckon?'

'A bloody Wilson, God damn it. You can bet that's a tinker. By heaven,' Tuck rumbled, 'I'll have them. One fine night I'll be waiting. I'll get square with the beggars.'

Hounding squalls drubbed the folds and Shep's dogs kept their heads down. But at dusk the rain lifted and, later that evening, Tuck took Zac to the covert. They could hear the sheep bleating. Far off, a fox called and once, faint on the night air, the man heard explosions.

More bombing. There was no rest for some, Tuck thought; the raids were relentless. They were lucky to miss them. 'Seek on, dog,' he commanded. An owl wailed in the timbers. Zac paused by the fowl huts.

Rose had shut the flaps tightly and cleared the nest-boxes. From the roosts came low cackles, sounds of stirring and preening. The odour stuck in Tuck's nostrils: sharp nitrogenous droppings. The spoor of rats told of visitors. They had scavenged the dung-boards but were gone at that moment.

Gun on arm, he stood waiting. From the shadows he listened as duck flighted over, a skein in the moon's glow. Some, he thought, would be gleaning where a field stood unploughed, grain abroad in the stubble. It was quiet, deeply peaceful, a night free of searchlights.

'What's that?'

Zac had growled. All Tuck heard was leaves dropping, the long soft sigh by the wood where the ash trees shed early. But the dog was alert. 'Go see,' Tuck whispered, moving. Ahead, the mongrel ran swiftly. 'Find the beggar; we'll have him!'

Something roused in the covert. Tuck could make out twigs snapping, the sounds of hasty departure. Heavily, he barged forward. It was dark in the ash poles. He followed Zac's noisy onrush, with gun cocked. Then, abruptly, the moon gleamed.

Across the glade, a low bear-like form scampered, its rolling gait clumsy. Tuck sat down on a tree stump. 'Let it be,' he said tiredly. The dog ran on a short way but the badger had vanished.

Steve returned for the beet-carting. The task was urgent, for the ground had softened. Already, wheels were knave-deep, bogged in mud and the cut leaves of sugar-beets. Clay-gaitered, Tuck pitched the roots to the carts with increasing haste.

Di led the horses. They needed coaxing as the loads grew, often too much for one, when a trace-horse was added to help through the morass. She waved at Steve and he nodded; they had had no chance yet to talk, for her father was near her. The big man bent and straightened. Roots drubbed on the cart-boards.

Zac shunned the brown porridge. Beside the lane, where the beet-tip was mounting, awaiting road-haulage, he sat on the tarmac, the wind in his ears. It was raw and he grumbled, nipping mud from a dew-claw. At length, the dog sought the hedge, settling down by the nose-bags the horses had emptied.

'That's a load.' Tuck let the blunt-pronged fork trail and went to the next cart. He toiled on, scarcely pausing.

Di urged the burdened mare forward. At first, the creature pulled gamely, flanks creasing with effort, then was stopped as the wheels sank. The girl watched Steve fetch the trace-horse. She frowned as he neared her.

'Well?' she questioned.

He scowled. 'It's a swamp, this.'

'Oh, this – how was London?'

'Bad,' he said. 'At night the docks blazed like straw-fires.'

'Steve, you went for selection.' She blew on cold fingers. 'What happened?' She glanced at her father, at Tuck's wide, swinging shoulders. 'He can't hear us,' she prompted.

51

Steve said, hitching the traces, 'They asked if I had a girl, Di.'

His reflective grin riled her.

'Is that anyone's business?'

'They asked us some odd ones.'

'Did you pass, for the Lord's sake?'

'Don't know.' His nose was blue; his feet mud-caked. 'They'll be writing . . .'

'No *inkling*?'

She swore as the mare trod on her boot. 'Hell, gid-up!' The pain seared. Di yanked her foot free, ill-tempered, and they moved with the team, at arm's length from the horses. Steve tried her patience. She had missed him, but now, in the flesh, he was irksome.

He led on the trace-horse. The team threw its weight forward, heads down, nostrils flaring. The girl was squelching and stumbling, splashed with muck as the hooves sloshed.

The laden cart lurched and shuddered. They charged the gate in great heaves, almost raising a canter, to run the sea of brown slime where the ground had been pounded.

On the lane, metal sparked. Next thing, they had halted and Steve tossed sacks on the horses, whose lathered flesh trembled. Di wiped mud from her cheeks. The stuff dripped from wheel-rims, from axles and hot bellies.

She said, 'You must have a *notion* – you didn't sleep through the tests, Steve?'

'They were stiff.'

Tuck came over, his face raw. Blobs of soil flecked a beard he had not shaved since Sunday. 'We'll do it,' he encouraged. 'More rain's coming but we'll get the lot carted.' His eyes were brilliant, triumphant, Di reckoned, as he and Steve tipped the cart, shooting its load on the verge where the trucks would collect it.

'Tell you later,' Steve grunted.

'Tell her *what*?' Tuck said, squinting.

'Never *you* mind,' Di answered.

She and Steve housed the horses. It was evening and the

field had been cleared. When the beet had been processed, its bulk, less the sugar, would return to the farm as a food for the cattle. It was a valuable siege crop notwithstanding the problems. As Di sieved chaff she tossed a scoop of oats on it.

'I'm not sorry that's over.'

'Wrong land for beet,' Steve said. 'He wouldn't grow it in peacetime. Muck and horses,' he muttered. He had stripped to his shirt and was rubbing sweat from the beasts with wisps of straw tightly twisted. 'He should buy a new tractor; work's never-ending with these brutes.'

'Damn your tractors.' Di took the sieve to a manger and the mare whinnied softly. 'In that mud they'd have floundered.' Down the stalls, raised heads watched her. They had, she thought, a sweet patience that was not her own virtue.

'Well, come on then, Steve, *tell* me!'

Zac had sprawled in the bedding, warm now, an ear listening. He was content in the stable, at peace with its inmates. In the gloom, lamp flames twitched, filling the horse-scented barn with immense prowling shadows.

Steve paused, his hair dishevelled. He said, 'It's taught me a lesson. I should have worked back at school when the chance was there. Would have done a sight better.'

'You think you *should* have done better?'

'Could have used twice the time. The maths was a beggar.'

'Same for all.' She fed another horse, asking, 'What did *they* say, the rest? Did they all find it tricky?' She tried to make it off-hand. She could see Steve was anxious.

He stooped, cleaning a hoof and picking at its recesses. 'Some,' Steve told her. 'There was a few like myself, chewing ends of the pencils. Most were bushy-tailed beggars with plenty of chat.' He kicked the muck away, turning so the light struck his glum features. 'Educated, not bumpkins.'

'Bah!' she said. 'Where's the rock-salt? Rock-salt's gone from this manger.'

'You could see *them* as pilots.'

Sparrows scuffed in the roof. Zac observed them with drowsy eyes – and the moth round the storm-lamp. When day broke, the birds would forage the standings, hopping under the horses. He pondered Tuck's oils and unguents. They stood by the bins, bottles smothered with cobwebs – cures for galls, coughs and lameness. Only Tuck knew the contents, some prescribed by old carters of his own father's farm days.

Di said, 'Chat won't fly Spitfires. You wait ...'

Steve admired her. Her hair was lank – as lank as she was robust – her strong face streaked with field dirt. At length, he said, 'If I *did* pass, you and me ...'

'Steve, I'm hungry.'

He watched the dog stretch, his gaze knowing. All the horses were eating, but Zac's belly was empty.

'Come on,' Di said. 'It's our turn.' Interrupted, Steve followed. Outside the girl closed the doors. Thin cold rain pierced the darkness.

10

He was there again, saying nothing, standing motionless, staring. Unsure how to take him, the dog stared back. There was no movement to challenge, no aggression to echo. Just the pale intent eyes which, once before, had outfaced Zac.

In the coombe, he had run, perplexed by the spectre. Now, in the shed, the dog froze. The gloom blunted the figure. It stood back from the door amid old apple boxes and the black dung of barn owls. Zac had come after rats; the silent stranger surprised him.

He could hear the bull scuffling. Behind the shed, the beast grunted, chomping hay in confinement. Outside, Rose was calling. He dithered. The man made no movement. Again, the mongrel retreated, tail down, glancing backwards.

Rose came by, thickly muffled, for the wind had turned and was icy. She wore a woollen hood and mittens, her coat padded with jumpers. She carried two buckets of eggs, just collected. Grounding them, she shrilled tersely, 'Come away from that bull; don't you pester that devil!'

Resting briefly, she advanced.

'He'd have you, dog, soon as blink. He'll have somebody one day.' Rose trudged on to the house. Still uneasy, Zac followed. Once, he stopped, looking round. The yard was empty. Indoors, Rose reached the kitchen and, lowering the buckets, called, 'Don't get set by that fire, Zac, I'm as perished as you are!'

She hung her coat in the passage. In a while she returned, hustling him from the hearth to stand, skirt hitched, her thighs warming. 'Lord,' she murmured, 'that's better.'

Zac sat upright, nerves edgy. Somewhere, windows were shaking, chastised by the weather. Draughts moaned. They made the parlour fire roar, slicing through from the back where the buckets of eggs stood. The wind made the dog jumpy. 'Be still,' Rose told him, 'it's nothing.' But he growled, not so certain.

A latch clicked

Cold air filled the passage, then the dog heard the door shut. Rose stiffened. Tuck and Di had the truck out; Steve was with the Case, ploughing. Zac bristled. He saw the man in the kitchen, tall and still, his eyes searching. The grey figure came forward.

As it did, it said, '*Sitze*,' gaze on Zac, voice compelling. '*Setze dich*.' Rose drew back.

'Please,' the man said, now in English, 'don't be frightened. See, your dog has sat quietly. He makes friends. A dog can tell, don't you think so?'

'Who are you?' Rose countered.

Trust Tuck to be working!

The man moved towards the shotgun. It was not, she thought, loaded. The shells were kept in the sideboard. But the stranger ignored it, hands stretched to the fire, his form wrenched by a shudder. '*Gott*, it's cold!' He half-smiled at the mongrel.

'We've met before; the dog knows me. On the farm,' he recounted.

The egg-thief, she reckoned. There was mud on his topcoat, the uniform crumpled. He was young, his face looked frozen, and she guessed he was hungry. A cold, hungry German. 'Shot down.' His teeth chattered. 'I slept rough but it's bitter.'

He trembled – the first German she had seen. The first foreigner, Rose thought. She said, 'You speak English ...'

'I was here as a student.'

'Oh,' she breathed, as the wind droned, speeding chill, tumbling leaves. Her quick temper ruffled, she said, 'I don't call it clever, sleeping out in this weather.'

'I hoped to get to your coast.'

Tuck's wife studied the airman, her emotions in turmoil. Stunned at first, she felt pity and a billowing outrage. By what right had he intruded? He might now appear harmless but he had come to harm England.

56

He shrugged, reading her mind.

'You have a phone? You should use it. If you call your police, they will send out an escort. Forgive me ...' He slumped at the table. When she had phoned, he looked deathly. Shamed, she ran to the kitchen.

He could as well have been Roy, and she thought, 'I must feed him.' There was soup on the stove. 'It's still warm,' she said. 'Drink it.'

'Thank you. I felt bad.'

'You'll revive.' She brought bread and poured milk. 'You've not eaten much lately.'

'Raw eggs.'

'I know,' Rose said.

He looked up, his eyes guilty. 'I'd like to pay for the eggs but ...' He spread his hands, looking sheepish.

'You brought bombs and not money!'

'Bombs?' The young man's face brightened. 'No,' he said, 'I've not bombed you. My squadron flies fighters. No bombs.'

Rose frowned sternly. He was no more than a lad; younger even than Steve. She said, 'The soldiers are coming, but they've a fair drive to get here. They'll see that you're sheltered.'

The young flier stiffened. He had gone to the window and turned, his eyes thoughtful. 'You have space here and good earth. I'd like that when the war ends – land to farm. And a dog.' He regarded Zac fondly. 'My uncle's a farmer, by the Rhine. As a child I would stay there, walking over the marshes with just such a mongrel.'

Rose sighed. 'When the war ends ...'

'It must wait.'

'At least you're safe,' Tuck's wife told him. She looked away, again softening. She would not like Roy captured. The thought of caged men was chilling. 'Time passes,' she blustered.

'Yes.' He smiled. 'There'll be peace before Christmas.'

'Christmas!'

'Well, spring at latest. When you get rid of Churchill. It's

57

wrong that we fight, you and us, Saxon people. We could achieve much together. We will when the war ends.' He stopped and Rose heard the soldiers. She was not sure he had meant it – he seemed to think they were beaten.

The room filled like a barracks.

A corporal grinned as he passed her. 'Blimey, missus, you live here? It's Siberia, this is.'

She stepped back, saying nothing. Tuck barged in with the escort. The trucks had turned up together. 'Ma!' Di's voice pierced the clatter. 'What in God's name is happening?' They shoved into the parlour. It seemed to Rose like a madhouse, thick with the drab khaki presence of men in battledress. Zac nudged her, his nose damp.

She felt saddened. The boy was still there but distant, no longer confiding. Now, his bearing was formal, the pale features rigid.

'You all right?' Tuck was saying. 'You sure you're all right, lass?'

'I'm all right.'

They were going. She did not know the boy's name and she had not asked where he lived. She might, she thought, have done that much, but now there were men at his shoulders. 'The soup was good,' he said gravely. 'You've been good to me, thank you.' He considered the mongrel. 'And you,' he said, smiling. 'I was afraid you might bite but I guess you speak German!'

'He does most things,' Rose muttered.

It grew louder. The roar filled the grey vacuum. The aircraft plunged lower. A fire was flaring, the dog's panting strident. Zac awakened, his chest heaving. The room was quiet, the hearth warm and Rose said, 'Well, move back then, you're too hot. You've been dreaming.'

'I'll let him out,' said the farmer.

Zac went to the shed. He examined the boxes. For a while he explored but there was nobody there and he trailed to the warren. There was mist in the bottom. The wind had ranted off south, leaving trees wrapped in mizzle, a dripping depression through which day barely glimmered. Ricks and gates were enveloped.

The stranger's scent had long faded.

Di had huffed, 'Can you beat it! They come to blow us to blazes and we serve up soup for them!'

'He was a lad,' Rose had told her.

'An enemy, Mother.'

'He wasn't Hitler or Goering. I was here; you were out, miss.'

Tuck had slapped his wife's bottom and grinned when she cuffed him. 'B'God, they'll give you a medal! You kept your head,' he applauded.

'Put my trust in Zac's instinct. He'd have gone for a ruffian.'

Now, the dog searched the thickets. A plane droned and he quaked, but the sound quickly faded. He was alone in the hollow. The mist had spread and grown dense; the nearby trees were merely shadows. There was no sign of the German. As he searched, Zac heard steps on the lane and followed warily.

Their drag was eerie. He heard the squeak of a bearing. A child whined and was told, 'Stop your bleating,' in a tone fraught and female. It swam in the vapour. 'I'm tired and sick of your snivelling.'

Damply, Zac overhauled them.

He knew the voice from the hutment. Their shapes blotched the drizzle, but he knew the thin, forlorn woman and the gnome-shape beside her. She was shoving a pram – a thing fit for the scrapyard – borne down by potatoes, a hundredweight sackful. One wheel shrieked as it turned. Without warning, it crumpled.

'Oh, my Christ!'

The dog crouched, watching quietly. From the murk came her sobbing, the same gulping anguish he had heard on the heath. The small boy clutched her skirt. 'Oh, my Christ,' wailed the woman again, her figure mourning the wreckage. 'That's it, the wheel's buckled.'

Di pulled up in the Morris. She had crawled through the

59

fog, trucking feed to Tuck's steers.

'Sal Wilson?' she shouted. 'Where the hell have *you* come from?'

'Murton village ...'

'You're soaked!' Di climbed down from the cab. 'You're both soaking!' She viewed the pram and the potatoes. 'You're in a fine pickle, aren't you?'

The woman moaned, shoulders heaving, and Tuck's daughter embraced her. The thin wet clothes were like membrane; Di could feel the bones through them. 'He won't come back. It's been months. He's lying dead in France somewhere.'

'You don't know,' Di was saying, her arm round the woman. 'He might be a prisoner.'

'The best of the Wilsons; the only one in the forces. He was good to me, Tom was. The best – and he's taken. Holy Mother ...'

'Come on, there's the child, Sal. Poor fellow, he's weary.'

Di's voice brought Zac forward. As she stooped to the infant, he charged, brisk with greeting. The child screamed.

'Call him off, miss!'

'For God's sake, he's friendly. Here, let the boy stroke him.'

Zac made much of the toddler. Both were wet, the dog's coat slick with moisture, his tail flicking water. The muddy snout nosed the boy, who looked doubtful then cackled, his face smudged where Zac licked it. 'There you are,' Di said gently, 'no harm in that, is there?'

Sal protested. 'The bog cur ...'

'Rubbish!'

'We know him. You don't know where he comes from. No good come from those parts.' The woman's eyes darkened. They swerved from Zac to the infant, then back to the mongrel.

Di said, vexed by the topic, 'He's Dad's. Zac's the farm dog.'

'Until the creature goes missing. I've seen him. We've all seen the bog cur. The devil calls and he answers, sneaks back

60

to the forest, the bogs where he came from. The devil's glades. I'd not trust him.'

Di exclaimed, 'Get on home, Zac.' She sat the child in the truck. 'I'm running up to the heath first. I can't leave them stranded.' She threw the pram on the Morris and raised the potatoes. Zac watched as she struggled. She said, 'You heard what Sal called you. Besides, you're too muddy.' Di started the engine.

'God bless you,' Sal told her.

'You were lucky I passed.'

The girl peered through the vapour. The tinker woman sat forward, child huddled against her. 'They'd have killed me,' she rasped. 'If I'd lost the potatoes, they'd have killed me, the Wilsons.'

11

The steers plunged down the meadow, Zac barking behind them. Tuck held the gate open. 'Yip-yip, gid-on, move 'em!' He turned the beasts for the farm. 'Hi-yi!' Turf was flying. They hit the lane in a bundle, flanks jostling, horns jabbing. They were heady, rumbustious. 'Gid-on, damn it!' It was time they were in now.

Zac chivvied their fetlocks. The pounding legs were mud-covered, as if togged out in stockings. Kicking back at the mongrel, the beasts bucked and clamoured, hooves drumming the tarmac. Zac dodged, his voice staccato. Tuck went with them, coat flying, leaving the gate to his daughter, who closed it.

She paused, an arm on the toprail. The dog sped like a bird, light and dark as he turned – like a dunlin, it struck her. Poor Sal! Zac had scared her, thought Di, as she followed the others. Tuck was bustling, gesticulating in openings, out-bawling the bullocks. She liked to see him work cattle; he caught their moods, the exuberance.

'Yip-yip-yip ...'

The beasts scrimmaged. Zac bounded, tail streaming. 'Steady up,' Tuck instructed. 'Hold 'em, dog, we're in traffic!' A lone car nosed towards them. The small Vauxhall gleamed brightly, its headlamps black-hooded, and the steers stopped to ogle. More accustomed to farm carts, they snuffled the driver.

'Morning, Wilf.' He inched forward.

'Doc ...'

Di nodded. Steaming beasts crowded round them. She found the old doctor seedy. 'You looked chilled,' she told him.

'*Anno domini*, Dinah.' The whiskers he sported were nicotine-tinted. 'Overdue for retirement. Ought to be somewhere fishing.' He nudged the car through the bullocks. 'I hear he's still overworking.'

'Hear *what*?' Tuck asked loudly.

'Overworking,' Di shouted.

'You've got a mule for a father.' The amusement was acid. 'Man's a fool,' said Doc Benson. He revved to scatter the livestock. 'I sympathize with your mother.'

'Aye, you would,' Tuck scoffed roughly. 'She picks you out double-yolkers. She keeps you in breakfasts.' Rose had a soft spot for Benson. Tuck scowled. 'Damned if I would.'

The car lurched on.

'Hi, dog, move 'em!' Zac collected a laggard and Tuck advanced, his arms lofted. 'Yip-yip!' His stride lengthened. 'Damned quack,' growled the farmer. They were nearing the farmhouse. He cursed, hustling forward. The wicket was open.

'Keep 'em out, Zac, get forrard!'

Zac hurdled the fencing. Skirting Rose's small garden, he reached the path and, lip curling, held the breach while the herd passed. Tuck drew breath, caught short-winded. He could have run all day, one time, now he got breathless quickly. Not that he would tell Benson.

They drove the beasts to the midden, looking on as they settled. Tuck leaned on the railing. He dropped a hand to the dog's head. Steers were butting and milling, scuffing up the straw litter. He had the mongrel for running – best drover in Hampshire. 'They'll do, girl,' he grunted. 'They'll do there for the winter.'

Di mooched off, her thoughts ranging. She felt sad for Sal Wilson. How would Sal do that winter? Di had scarcely known Tom but Sal was pathetic. Di pitied the child. She found Steve at the lean-to. 'Any news?' she demanded.

Di could tell in an instant. He had the plugs from the Case and swung round, his hands oily. Steve was happy with engines but his smug glint was special. The jolt she felt inside startled her; she was not prepared for it. 'You've passed?'

He said, 'Aircrew.' He balled the rag he was holding and flung it above him. 'Aircrew, Di; I've made aircrew!'

63

'So much for your gloom, Steve.' She controlled herself quickly. She was not in love with him.

'Mind, I've still got the training.' He stooped and picked up the oil rag. 'You can fail on the training.'

'God . . .'

'Oh, not that I mean to.' He wiped his hands, grinning. Taking the plugs to his toolbox, he worked on the carbon. 'Up to me,' he said firmly; 'no excuses now, are there?' He inspected the plug-head. 'I'll be sorry to leave, Di.'

'It's your choice.'

'If I'd thought . . .'

'Steve, I told you.'

'Aye, you did.' He smiled slowly. 'I took your word and I done it. Hard to reckon it happening. Me – up there. By accounts it's a dazzler – summer all the year round – when you're through those old storm clouds.' He paused then asked, 'Will you write, then?'

The girl drawled, 'Not if *you* don't.'

'I'll write.' He blew hard on the spark-plug. 'There'll be plenty to tell you. Di, it's you, like I said . . .'

'Yes.' She made it sound brittle.

Tuck had gone to the hayrick. He tramped back to the midden, a load on his shoulders. Man and fork were enveloped. Askance, Steve watched the farmer. He said, 'The worst bit's not over; I'm letting your dad down. He won't take it lightly.'

'Too late for cold feet.'

'I feel badly.'

Di shrugged. 'Roy felt badly, but he made his decision. It's your affair. War's no picnic.' Not by a long chalk, she brooded – wasting her prime on Tuck's bullocks! 'We've all got our problems. He'll have to hire a new hand.'

'To take care of this lady.' Steve thumped the Case fondly. Twisting a rag round a finger, he cleaned the threads on the engine then screwed back the spark-plugs. 'Roy did right,' he reflected. 'He got in. I admire him.' He opened the fuel tap. With a smile, he said, '*Contact!*'

Di watched as he cranked and the tractor fired smoothly.

He stood back, his gaze lofted. The girl eyed the midden.

The farmer led out the bull. Frost had whitened the yard and the beast's feet left hoof-marks. The dog kept his distance. Zac crouched near the wall, his rump to the granite, his dorsal hairs shafting. The cold pierced, scythe-sharp, and numbed the dog's flattened belly.

The bull nosed the hoar-frost. Warm from its box, the beast snorted. 'Easy,' Tuck told the monster, 'watch your step, you old beggar.' The voice was confident, soothing, but Zac remained watchful. He saw Steve leave the dairy and cross the lane, his boots black on the rime, his nose ruddy.

'Need a hand?'

'Break the ice, boy.' Tuck held the nose-lead two fisted. 'Break the ice on the trough.'

It cracked loudly.

The crunch stirred the great animal, who slouched to the water, dwarfing Zac. In the chill, far-spread pallor, it held dominion, imperious, baleful. The dog was mistrustful. The bull's appearance was slothful, each lazy move pondered. Yet Zac had seen it move quickly, its temperament fickle.

Steve braced. 'I'd like a word with you, boss.' He spoke nervously.

Zac's ears cocked. The bull had snuffled the water and stamped, undecided. 'When he's back,' Tuck said gruffly, 'when I've got him inside, lad.'

The bull swilled the liquid. His small, vein-shot eyes swivelled, scrutinizing the mongrel.

'What's the girl up to?' Tuck asked.

'Grinding cake for the cattle. When we've spoken, I'll help her.'

Tuck grunted. He turned the bull from the trough. It slewed slowly, thirst sated, a great dewlap swinging, as Zac saw the ice patch. Steve's mouth had half opened. Already, Tuck's foot was sliding. He went down with an oath, boots and gaiters upended, his arms spread, and the bull roared.

Steve tried to distract it. The thought of Rose crossed his mind; her fear of the creature. Tuck had brushed off her

65

warnings. Now the beast was above him, its head lowered, horns raking. It seemed to Steve scarcely real. Reality was the Air Force, not this lumbering shorthorn and the man trapped beneath it.

'Keep clear!' Tuck rolled sideways. 'Run, lad!' the man shouted.

Zac was snarling. The dog had slipped closer. As the horns jabbed, he sallied. Whirling, Zac rushed the monster, snapping at the bull's muzzle. Spittle flew from the mongrel. His mask was ferocious. Tuck gained time to draw backwards. 'Stand clear; watch the beggar!'

But Steve was pounding a flank, fists driving at bull-hide. Zac yelped. Swept to the wall, the dog whimpered. Steve saw Tuck grab the nose-chain. At last, the big man was up, holding on, swearing softly. 'Come on back . . . steady, damn you . . .' The crooning was breathless and seemed to last for an aeon. Then the vast beast, still trembling, was inched to its compound.

'He's in – shoot the bolt, lad.'

'You all right?' Steve said, shaken.

'Aye, boy, where's the dog?'

Steve cast round him, uncertain. They found Zac by the wall and Tuck knelt to the mongrel. The frosted stone glinted bleakly. 'Zac?' Tuck cupped the head gently. The tongue was loose; the eyes, sightless. The man said, 'He's alive.'

'He was walloped.' Steve bent down. 'He looks bad.'

'Blamed fool,' Tuck said fiercely. 'The blamed fool got between us, took the damage. Call the vet, lad – indoors.' He looked up. 'No, forget it. He'll be out. Fetch the Morris.' He cradled the mongrel. They put the dog in the cab, a limp form on the floor, and Steve watched the truck vanish.

Wilf Tuck jabbed his foot down. Iced fields filled the windows, the ridged soil set like concrete. In the kale, a stooped cowman, his damp apron frozen, was swinging a sickle. Tuck sped on in the rocking truck. 'Damned dog! Damned old mongrel!' He yanked his cap forward. Diamond-cold, the light dazzled. Black copses rose in it, and the hearth-smoke of Murton.

66

He flung the truck through the village. Zac's head had lolled sideways, an upturned eye staring. Past the pond fumed the Morris; past the shop and Steve's lodgings. Tuck spotted the Vauxhall. It was parked by the forge and he stopped the truck near it. 'Is he here?' he asked Rutter.

'With Flo,' said the blacksmith. He was repairing a horse-hoe, its metal red on the anvil as he plied his hammer. He said, 'The flu – she's been low.' Dirt scorched as sparks tumbled. Tuck growled, looking past him.

Benson came from the cottage. 'Trouble, Wilf?' he said, squinting. He smelled of Scotch. 'Not the women?'

'The dog,' said Tuck. 'In the Morris.'

Doc Benson lost interest.

'Laid out. The bull caught him.'

Rutter doused the hot metal. Above the sizzle of water, he said, 'I'm sorry to hear it. Yon mongrel was clever.'

'Clever?' Tuck snarled. 'A godsend! Don't just stand there, Doc, damn you!'

Doc Benson, looking jaded, lit a part-smoked John Player's. The cigarette glimmered and his bleary eyes ranged the farmer. Doc Benson was shock-proof. In a life of rural practice, he had cut ulcers from horses, bandaged cats, revived piglets. 'Blast your dog, Wilf, where is he?'

They went out to the street.

Rutter glanced at Tuck, smiling.

'*That's* a sick dog?' leered Benson.

Zac was up on a seat, his head through the cab window. When he saw them, his tail thumped. 'I'll be damned,' Tuck said feebly. His face creased. 'I'll be hell-damned!' He drove back, grinning broadly. 'You thick-skulled beggar,' he bellowed. 'You might have been crippled. You had me worried a moment, by God you did!'

It was still freezing that evening. The bombers went to the Midlands. Rose heard them pass, motors throbbing, as she scrubbed the day's eggs and set aside half-a-dozen, soft-shelled and misshapen. The news would come later: towns wrecked, convoys battered. There was no joy on the wireless;

people lived on defiance – and a fresh egg when lucky.

'Lord, it's cold,' gasped Tuck's daughter.

The girl washed hands rough from farm work; her face strained, Rose reckoned, dulled by lack of amusement. Life was dull in the black-out: no young men, dances, pictures. At Di's age, Rose had rollicked, led Tuck and the others a merry chase.

'Where's your father?'

'Steve had something to tell him.'

'So have I,' Rose said sharply. 'That bull's got to go, Di.' She had warned the man often. There was enough daily anguish without needless danger. 'The brute's had him over. It's not staying on this farm!'

Di went into the parlour. 'Steve said the dog saved them.'

'This time,' Rose commented. She piled food in the dog's bowl. Zac had come in with Di and was waiting with hungry eyes. Rose ladled a bonus which was quickly demolished. 'Tuck's a fool,' growled the woman. 'He dotes on those shorthorns. You wait, girl, I'll tell him!'

'Ma ...' Di paused. She watched the fire move the shadows.

'Well?'

'Go easy,' Di told her.

Rose advanced from the kitchen. She crossed her arms, her gaze inquiring.

Di shrugged. 'Ma, Steve's leaving.' She shoved her hands in her pockets. 'Going into the Air Force. He's telling Dad at this moment.'

Rose confronted the fireplace and stared into the embers. At length, 'I guessed,' she said dourly. The boy had kept to himself; avoided meeting her, lately. She eyed the snapshot of Roy that was propped on the mantel. 'They're all going,' she brooded. 'Steve was bound to leave sometime. He stayed this long for you.'

'Dragged his feet.'

'Will you miss him?'

'Won't we all?' the girl parried. She was unsure of her emotions. 'Poor Dad, he'll be livid.'

68

'There'll be worse,' Rose said grimly. 'If that's the worst that's to happen before we're through, we'll be lucky.' She smoothed her skirt, and thrust her chin forward. 'Turn the lamp up, it's gloomy. And stir the fire, girl – that's no fire for your father. And Zac, just you settle. He'll be in, the great numskull. Don't *you* reckon on leaving us yet awhile!'

Part Two

TOWARDS VAAGSO

1

He had a week: his first leave from the squadron. A mackerel sky flared above and the heat popped the gorse pods along the familiar lanes. Beneath an elm, cattle rested, their heads to the tree's bole. Their tails swung at insects. Steve could see Brindle's heifer, grown large since last summer, and beyond her the buildings.

A lad came from the farmstead, leading a cart-horse. Steve paused and shoved his cap back. The old mare shook her bridle. It jangled, brass shining and, as Steve ambled forward, the lad gazed at his tunic. 'How-do, Jim,' Steve said brightly. The boy blushed. 'It *is* Jim, the blacksmith's nephew? I heard you've settled down well, Jim.'

'Aye.' The youngster was burly. He said, 'It's all right, is farm work,' swiping a fly from his forehead. The mare was champing. 'Sooner be in *your* boots, though – an air-gunner!'

Steve smiled. He said drily, 'I'd sooner be up front, driving, but you can't have it all – case of where you fit best, Jim.' The smile dimmed. He thought, *Jammed into a turret, your bloody knees quaking*! He eyed the house. 'Is the boss in?'

'Laid up. He's been poorly.'

'*Laid up?*'

Tuck scorned ailments.

'On his back,' Jim said calmly, a man used to problems. 'And the dog's gone,' he added. It was stale news, he reckoned; an air-gunner eclipsed it. 'What plane do you fly in?'

Steve was moving already. 'A bag o' nails,' he called back and, with a grin, reached the buildings. He could hear the bull guzzling. He grinned again, now more broadly; Tuck had not been defeated. He looked round, memories flooding: ploughing, threshing, spud-lifting – climbing trees after pullets.

'My, they turn you out smartly!' Rose threw the door open. 'And plump! They don't starve you.'

'It's the beer!' Steve informed her.

'Come in. Rest your legs, then.'

They sat in the parlour. It was strange, Steve thought vaguely, his first time past the kitchen. The room was fresh, full of knick-knacks. Rose had snatched off her apron. She fluffed the hair at her nape, a dimpled elbow swept upwards. 'Steve, it's real good to see you!' Her welcome was chatty. For a time, she asked questions, amused by his jargon, but he sensed she was worried.

'How's Di?'

'Tired, I reckon. Scarcely pauses,' Rose told him. 'She's getting more like her father. You know he's been ill, Steve?' Now the strain was less hidden. 'Went down without warning.' Hands clasped, she sat forward. 'Went down like a bullock, as if he'd been pole-axed.'

'Overwork?' Steve conjectured.

'So we thought. I'll make tea; you'll be thirsty. The doctor says its pneumonia. Means a long rest, whatever.'

'That won't suit Mr Tuck.'

Steve examined the parlour. It smelled of flowers and wax polish – a far cry from the squadron and the smell of the Blenheims. Rose had put out her wasp traps, the jars of jam-sweetened water, and scraped down the fire-back.

'Of course,' she said, 'he won't have it. Says he'll be up to harvest. Mind, he can't cross the bedroom but that's what he'll tell you. Have some cake,' Rose persuaded. 'You must go up and see him. He's asleep now, but later ...'

There was a picture of soldiers propped up on the mantel

and Steve saw Roy with them. There was a ship's rail, snow and a jetty – Commandos at Lofoten. The raid had bolstered the nation, refreshed battered spirits. It seemed a pinprick at this stage, as Hitler smashed Russia.

'Wish I'd known,' Steve said, munching. 'I'd have brought the boss something.'

'All he wants is that dog, Steve. Damn the dog, always roaming.' Rose thumped down the teapot. 'There's always trouble when Zac goes. God knows where he gets to.'

'I'll look.'

'Di's been looking.'

He found the girl with the Morris. She was swinging the handle, quietly cursing the engine. 'It's flooded,' he told her.

'Damn the cow,' she said hotly. 'I meant to collect you.'

Steve beamed.

'Well, don't stand there.' She scowled, caught dishevelled. 'Come on then, *you* start it, since you're here,' she said, flustered.

He laughed. She looked marvellous, hair awry, her cheeks rosy. That was how he recalled her, the broad-spaced eyes shining. 'So you've missed me!' He watched her.

'Don't kid yourself,' Di said. 'Jim's as handy as you were.' She thought he looked handsome. 'Except,' she said, 'with a tractor, and *I* drive the tractor.'

Steve stepped to the truck. Soon, the engine was idling. 'Same old knack,' Di reflected, 'we'll find you some work, Steve.'

'Won't be hard, the corn's ready. You'll need help – your dad poorly. You didn't say ...'

'Been too busy.'

'I've a week,' Steve said briskly. 'Should do most of the harvest.'

'Don't be daft, I was teasing. You can't spend your leave working.'

'Want to bet?'

She said nothing, thumbs in her belt, her gaze searching. This was a new, forceful Steve, no longer uncertain. 'Try to stop me,' he challenged. He turned to the Morris. 'Well,' he said, 'you're the gaffer. I'm on – where we going?'

'To find Zac.'

'*I'll* drive,' Steve said.

He braked on the heath. The old cab was a furnace; the sun blazed on the roof and the engine heat stifled. Steve ballooned his cheeks, puffing. 'She's misfiring,' he grunted.

'That's the least of my worries.'

They got down and Di added, 'The binder's more vital.' She scanned the scrub for the mongrel. Her shirt had stuck to her back and her lank hair was sweaty. 'If that's crocked . . .'

'I'll soon check it. The binder's no problem. I'll see it's greased,' Steve said calmly.

'Thanks, Steve.'

'Piece of cake, Di.' They made for the hutment. 'Only take a jiff, don't you worry.' The heather was shadeless. He could see the rough ponies bunched away in the distance where a few spindly birches formed meagre oases. Fowls huddled in dust bowls. Di said, 'Christ, what a summer! It's not just Dad and the harvest, we're behind with the ditches and the hedges are dreadful.'

'They'll keep. Let's find Zac; he's the medicine the boss needs!'

'I'll ask Sal.'

'Sal?' Steve grimaced.

'It's a chance. She thinks Zac haunts the timbers.'

Di strode to the dwelling. A tin chimney protruded from the hut's rusting iron roof. Inside, it was dim, as confined as a brooder, all but one window boarded. A stove, enthroned on cracked concrete, held the central position, its flu a scorched column. At Sal's skirts, the child grizzled.

'You remember Steve,' Di said.

The child brightened. 'A pilot!'

Di smiled. 'An air-gunner.'

'What lazy boys become,' Steve said.

Sal took hold of the toddler. In the dimness, she glowered, regarding Steve with suspicion. 'Air-gunner?' She sniffed.

'Tom was killed,' she said darkly.

'Look, Sal ...' Di engaged her.

While they talked, Steve took stock, his discomfort increasing. The place was a shambles; it made him uneasy. His gaze flitted squeamishly from the shadows and the woman's sordid possessions, once more to the entrance. There, his eye was held briefly. The door was patched on the back by a light alloy panel whose scratched paint intrigued him. There were ragged holes in it.

'Come on, Steve.' Di was leaving.

He touched the scored metal.

'She says Zac's in the forest. She's heard howling at night. From the lumber trail, Sal says.' Di paused. Sal was watching. 'Full of tales,' Tuck's girl whispered, 'they're *all* superstitious. But we're here – shall we look?'

'Aye, let's go,' he said tersely.

They made for the timbers. 'Curse the dog,' Sal was shouting. Di walked on, Steve beside her. The tinker woman's voice followed. 'Let the bogs have the mongrel. You'll find no good through the trees, miss ...'

It grew cooler, more leafy. Di sighed, smiling faintly. 'Poor soul,' she reflected, 'she's scared of the forest: they all are, the Wilsons.'

They sought Zac, the man whistling. Now and then, they would holler, their yelps piercing the greenness which closed as they forayed. The track had grown sketchy. Briars cast spurs from its edges; brambles tangled with grasses. Thick now with fresh growth, the woodmen's clearing was silent, the white-mooned stumps amid herbage like tombs in a graveyard.

For a while, the two rested.

'Damned old hound ...'

Steve grinned glumly.

At length, the girl said, 'You made it. I mean, you made aircrew.'

'Aircrew but not pilot. The maths had me knackered. Never could fathom vectors ...'

'No regrets?'

'It's still flying.' Jammed in with the Brownings, the twist-grips, the ammo.

'Good for you!' Di led forward, past fire-blackened circles ringed by charred ends of branches. 'Zac!' she bawled. 'Damn the beggar.' They were back among timbers, in now trackless forest. 'Waste of time, Steve, I reckon.'

'Ground's soft. We're near bog land.'

A skein of steamy mist met them. Coming off the wet region, it crawled round the tree-roots and fingered through branches. Underfoot, it was soggy. On the floor of dark chasms, and where thorn had its enclaves, the first water trickled. Rills oozed through the ground growth.

Di said, 'This is what spooks them.' Great tree-vaults were fetid, grotesque where the mist stole, its shifting shapes eerie. 'This is why they won't come here.' The deep forest was dangerous. Wild ponies had perished, as had cattle which strayed there, sucked down in the quagmires.

Steve said doubtfully, 'Maybe. We don't *know*. Planes have crashed in this jungle. They're scrap to the Wilsons.' Like an alloy wing panel. 'A plane crash means pickings.'

'Grave robbing?'

'It happens. Scrap's gold to the Wilsons.'

Di had stopped. The mist drifted. It formed sombre grey eddies, opening over the morass, and the girl cried, 'The Spitfire! Look, Steve, in the bog!' She could see the tail section rearing out of the quagmire, an aileron creaking. 'My God, Steve, remember? That day in the 'taters ...'

'Aye,' breathed Steve. He felt clammy. He could still hear the engine, the scream as it nose-dived.

Di croaked softly, 'Poor beggar ...'

'He'll be deep.'

'God,' the girl said.

'Peaceful, Di.' He put an arm round her shoulders.

'Steve,' she said, 'let's go back.' She had turned from the wreckage. 'Zac's not here; he'd have heard us. Let's go back to the truck, Steve.'

2

Tuck was propped up on pillows. He looked old, his face fallen, loose and no longer boyish. The eyes peered from grey hollows. 'Where's Benson?' he mumbled.

'He's gone down,' Di said gently; 'he's downstairs with mother. Doc's left you more medicine.' Bottles littered the bedside. Steve had not seen so many, except in the stable, those dark with horse potions. He pitied the farmer.

Di had said, 'You won't know him.' Now, she watched Steve's jaw tighten, the cheek muscles flexing. His contrived brightness faltered, then was saved with an effort and, inside, Di applauded.

'Roy?' said Tuck.

'No, it's Steve, Dad.'

'Oh, that damned deserter.'

'That'll do,' Di reproved him.

A fly buzzed. It was sultry. Beyond Rose's cheery curtains, cows trekked to the dairy with udders full, their pace lethargic. Benson's car caught their interest and they stopped to stare, their ears flapping. Across the lane, ripe corn rustled, the hue of pie pastry, assailed by flocks of sparrows.

Tuck gave Steve a sly twinkle. 'Got guts, I'll say that, lad, going up in them nail-bags. I ought to have skinned you!'

'Thought you *would*,' Steve responded. 'That, or blow a damned gasket.'

The herd passed, save for stragglers. At its rear came Tuck's cowman, scowling under the window, lame-legged and arthritic, old as Shep and as captious. Tuck turned feebly to listen. 'They're late,' wheezed the farmer. 'The dog should've fetched them. Where's Zac?'

'He'll be back, Dad.'

'Back? Where is he?' Tuck whispered.

Di stood by the curtains. Doc Benson was leaving. Rose

had gone to the doorstep, her anxious voice floating upwards. 'He's still poor.' Then, reassured by the doctor, 'Thank God,' she said quickly, 'I had the chump buried!'

Benson coughed. 'Wilf's a mule. He'll pick up, Rose, he's stubborn.' He went to the Vauxhall.

Rose called out, 'Wait – your eggs, Doc.'

She put the eggs in the car and Doc Benson concealed them beneath a newspaper. 'Bless you, Rose. Keep him cheerful.' He took a nip from his hip-flask and reached for the starter. Di turned back from the window. Some hope, she reflected – Tuck cheerful not working!

'Blamed quack,' her dad muttered, 'only comes for a hand-out.'

'Don't be silly,' the girl said. Tuck's eyes closed. 'Just be grateful.'

'Where's Zac?' The lids flickered.

Doc Benson's car snorted and drew off, the sound fading, and Steve glanced at Tuck's daughter. His return had been timely. He pondered the Spitfire. He might still be a farmhand but for seeing the plane crash. It had stirred his emotions as Tuck's sickness now stirred them, and pitched his mind back to farming.

Di said, 'Rest, Dad, stop fretting.'

'Where's the dog, Di? I want him.'

'Tuck,' she rasped, 'you be patient.'

'Bah!' His head moved a fraction. 'I could die ...'

'No you won't. Benson says ...'

'Bloody Benson!' Tuck's vision was bleary. He guessed the damned quack had doped him.

'I'll be off,' Di said, moving. 'Things to do. Don't be long, Steve.' She touched his arm, leaving quickly. Tuck appeared to be drowsing. Steve gazed from the window. In the eaves, wasps were droning while swifts hawked the corn's brow in black tempestuous crescents. He regarded the hedges. She was right, they were scruffy – but at least out of Tuck's vision.

'Steve?' the farmer stirred slightly.

'Aye, I'm here,' Steve assured him.

'B'God, I've been clobbered. You ever took sick, Steve?'

'Not bad.'

'Mind you don't,' Tuck said, groaning. 'That's a rule to remember. Can't sit up; good for nothing. I'll not make the harvest.'

Or much else, Steve considered, this side of winter. The big man was a spectre. Steve had seen shot-up aircrews dragged from kites looking better. A plane crossed the sky-dome. Coastal recce, he figured. It passed on, vapour smudging, and Steve said, 'I'll be helping. You rest – I'll help out, boss.'

For a while, it was silent in the muggy farm bedroom. Then, 'Still there?' Tuck said feebly.

'Still here.'

'Come nearer.' Tuck raised his head with an effort an inch from the pillow, the strain showing in his features. Veins stood up at his temples. 'Steve, they're lying. The dog's dead, I can feel it.' He sank back again, breathless. 'They won't tell me,' he growled, 'but I know from their faces. This time, he's a gonner.'

'Zac?'

'Finished.'

'Come on, boss, Zac's not bought it. You know Zac – a survivor. He'll turn up, the old wizard.'

But, later, Rose was less sanguine. 'Time will come,' she predicted, 'when the creature stays missing. A stray's a stray, Steve, let's face it. I always pray it's the *next* time.'

'He'll be back.'

'We'll see,' Rose said.

Rose took drinks to the cornfield. It was a glittering morning, the turning sails of the binder shot with sun in the dust cloud. As they pushed the corn downwards, each cut was moved sideways, sheaved and bound on the conveyor. The machine clattered past her. 'Tea!' she bawled. The sails rested.

Steve wiped his oily hands, sweating. Di and Jim, snatching sheaves, were stooking them on the stubble. The long-strawed wheat bundled well – unlike barley, whose short sheaves were scruffy – but the work was back-breaking.

The stookers stretched, hot and thirsty. 'Cold tea,' Rose said, pouring. There was cider for later. Now, the mugs emptied quickly.

Di surveyed the lane, frowning. Where hedgeside weeds ripened, silver thistledown floated: more work in the making. She said, 'No sign of the cowman.' The hard ground was cracking, she noticed. 'Or bloody Shep,' she said sourly. 'I told the beggars we'd need them.'

'*Did* you, now?' Rose said grimly.

'It's too bad,' Di protested.

'I could find them,' Jim told her.

'Fat lot of notice they'd take, Jim!'

'Beggars!' Tuck's wife said quietly. 'They'll take notice, the beggars. Just you keep the rest working; I'll sort out the weasels!' She returned to the field gate, her feet crunching the straw stumps. Dusty burdock leaves crackled; cast aside by the reaper, they lay beside vole runs and relics of mouse nests. Soon, groundsel would sprout; scarlet pimpernel open.

Rose eyed the dense uncut hedges, wild with tansy and soapwort, strung with bryony berries. Her gaze fierce, she strode briskly. Weeds were thick in the turnips, the field due for hoeing. Di was doing her best. The girl worked like a Trojan and her mother's blood boiled to think the men were not helping.

She found them together. 'You're a fine pair!' Her voice lashed. 'Huddled here in a corner! You were told to go stooking.'

'By yon girl ...' The cowman shrugged his humped shoulders, his frame distorted by milking. His life had passed in chill dairies; the draughts were frozen in him, his old joints arthritic. 'You tell the girl, missus: I be paid for to milk, mind cows, not to harvest.'

'Aye,' croaked Shep, 'there's the difference.' He was wasted, a scarecrow. 'Ye'd best learn *her* the difference – twixt shepherd and farmhand.'

'Oh?' snarled Rose. 'High and mighty! Our elders and betters!'

'Old enough,' wheezed the cowman. His glare was defiant.

'Too old to need telling by yon chit in trousers.'

'Lord,' cried Rose, 'if Tuck heard you!'

'The boss knows the difference.' Shep smirked, saying slyly, 'In all the years I been shepherd, *he's* not put me to stooking. You ask him; he'll tell you.'

'I'd give you your cards first. If I was boss, you'd be packing!'

'Ah,' the cowman said slowly, used to threats of dismissal, 'but ye'd do your own milking. There's no men for hire, missus. War's a terrible curse, now.'

'Curse? I'm *twice* cursed, you beggars.' She checked the worst of her anger. There was no time for battles. More astutely, she added, 'I should think you're ashamed, letting womenfolk worry. How long have you known me – since I was the girl's age?' She watched their eyes flicker. They still found her bonny, with her arms bare to the shoulder, brown as hen's eggs and freckled. 'I've *depended* on you two. A bit of help through the harvest . . .'

'Well . . .' said Shep, looking awkward.

'It's finding time,' groused the cowman. 'Got to wash up the dairy.'

'Man, you're standing here smoking!' She watched them knock out their pipes. 'Baccy's short,' she reflected. 'I might find some of Tuck's.'

'Sweet, his flake is!' They wavered. 'We could help a *while*,' Shep said.

'Few hours,' said the cowman.

'Right,' snapped Rose, 'and don't dawdle.' The tone brooked no nonsense. 'I want you there quickly.'

When she took down the cider, they were stooped in the cornfield. 'Brought the baccy?' Shep wheedled and she smiled saying, 'Later. When the gathering's over.' Rose paused. 'That's *depending* . . .'

Di grinned. 'Soon be done here. Thank God for fine weather.' She palmed the grains from a wheatear. They were nut-hard, set golden. 'Going to be a good yield, Ma. That should cheer him indoors; take his mind off the mongrel.'

It was late when the work stopped. Di and Steve stayed the

81

longest, regarding their labours. Rabbits ran from the stooks. The pair watched them in silence, then Di said, 'No dog. He'd have caught us a supper.'

'He'll be catching his own now.'

'Unless someone else feeds him.'

'He'd not go with strangers.'

'I don't know,' Di said, puzzled, 'he liked that young German.'

Steve laughed. 'Sure – an airman!' He wiped his brow with his fingers. They left grubby striations. '*Everyone* loves an airman,' he said, his face candid.

'Steve . . .' The girl's glance was solemn. A bunting called at the laneside and, farther, a chiff-chaff, its short notes dissolving. 'Steve, I just want to thank you.' He held her shoulders and kissed her, his arms moving round her. There was no hesitation – unlike the last time, the girl thought. He seemed several years older. 'You're wrong, Steve.' In a twelvemonth! 'All the *nice* girls love sailors.'

'Not mine.' He smiled gravely, his lips sharp from her sweating. 'I meant it, Di, about us. I still mean it . . .' He broke off. 'Your ma's calling.'

'Time to eat. Hell, it's late.'

Rose had come to the field gate. She considered them, frowning. 'Food's been ready a half-hour.' Her eye met her daughter's. It switched to Steve. 'I've got plenty. You'll stay, lad?'

'Like this?'

'You can wash.'

'Left my kit at the lodging.'

'We're not grand,' Rose Tuck told him. 'It's not the sergeants' mess here, but we'll see that we fill you.'

'Then, thanks.'

Di was grinning. It was warm as the sun sank, and the house door, left open, compelled her attention. 'Look, the doorstep! Dear heaven . . .' There was mud on the granite. It led over the threshold, across the floor to the stairs: a distinct trail of pad-marks. They must have come from the pond, for the ground was baked solid.

82

Di was first to the landing. She took the stairs at a gallop, Rose and Steve close behind. 'Christ!' The girl's gasp alarmed them. All three peered at Tuck's room.

The bed was crumpled and filthy, its counterpane mud-soiled. Zac's tail revolved wildly. Thin, wet and bedraggled, he met them with rapture. Rose gazed at Tuck dumbly. He was sitting up straight-backed, his face delighted. At last, his laugh filled the bedroom; the laugh she had prayed for.

'Now we'll show them,' he cackled. 'You can sack your Doc Benson – Zac's home, I feel better! Hell,' he said as they goggled, 'don't gawp, feed the beggar. Poor hound, he'll be empty.'

'*Poor hound*?' Rose recovered. 'My bedspread, for God's sake!'

'Bit of mud,' Tuck retorted. 'Dog was hot; took a cooler.'

Steve looked at the women. They were moist-eyed, mouths open. The girl was laughing, he reckoned; either laughing or crying. Steve blinked. It was catching.

3

Zac sat with the farmer. Between whiles, he drove cows, dealt with rats, watched the buildings. The farm was safe, Tuck asserted, with the dog back on duty. 'More to rights,' he told Rose, making much of the mongrel, 'a different place.'

'Where *you* should be,' Rose snapped. He was downstairs in his pyjamas. 'Back to bed; Benson's calling.'

He touched the gun on the firebreast. 'Had enough of bed, woman.' There was dust on the gunstock. '*And* Doc Benson.'

'Put that gun down!'

'Needs cleaning.' Tuck glowered. He said, 'Play us a record – just one, Rose, since I'm better.'

'You're not cured, you're improving.' She deigned to play him *Run Rabbit*. 'Then to bed. You're not fit yet.' But he caught her and, cackling, swung her round, her skirt swirling. 'Tuck, get off ...'

The tune echoed.

'See – I'm strong, Rose; I'm better.'

Zac watched them, his ears cocked. The dog liked the music. His eyes followed them, glowing, alert to Tuck's pleasure, the warmth of the moment despite Rose's protests. Zac's gaze roamed the parlour: the gun, the knitting, and the curtains, dark-lined for the black-out, which framed the evening. Outside, the trees were loud with birdsong.

He stretched, his forelegs extended, and his brown eyes rolled slowly. He could hear the old Vauxhall and left as the car stopped.

'Damn it, Wilf, here's the doctor!'

Zac looked back.

They were talking. He heard Benson's, 'What's *this*, then?' and Rose say, 'I told him. He'll be out next thing, ditching. That, or hoeing the turnips. I told him you'd chide him.'

'I'll wash my hands of him first, Rose. If he *wants* a relapse ...'

'A paying farm,' Tuck corrected. 'It means working, Benson.'

'The man's a mule, Doctor.'

'Aye,' said Tuck, 'and I'm better. B'God, the girl's been a brick but she can't lift a twelve-stone nor geld a damned blackface. I'm needed.'

'Then you'd best obey orders.' Doc Benson's eye wandered. 'Been a dry sort of day, Rose.'

'Will you take a small whisky?'

Zac sloped off, his nose questing. The scent he caught was elusive but he followed, his pace quickening into a determined brisk lope. It led the dog past the dairy to broad copse-strewn country. The cropped fields were blackened, full of late-feeding rooks.

Four miles – five, slipped behind him; other farms loomed and dwindled, smells drifting from them. The lanes offered diversion but Zac's gait was steady, the keen snout selective. The sun was red when he paused, his quarry glimpsed on the brow. Head raised, Zac dogged the cyclists down the hill.

They had left the bikes at the back. The spin was bracing, a rare break for Di, who had put on a frock and felt good as they pedalled, Steve on Rose's bone-shaker. Its front mudguard rattled. He had clowned, wobbling daftly as they rolled through the country.

'Bloody Blenheims are safer!'

'You'll have me off, Steve, you numskull!'

She had squealed, swooping past him. For a while, her cares melted. The corn was cut, the sheaves carried. 'Come on, Steve, we'll be late and miss the newsreel. It's miles to the fleapit.'

Now, a small queue had gathered. Wives and girls clung to soldiers, some with eyes for Steve's tunic, with the single wing on it. The cashier quizzed him coolly. 'Two rear stalls?' She paused, adding, 'You can't take that dog in.'

'Dog?'

The couple turned slowly. The mongrel had joined them. 'I left him home,' Di said, groaning. 'Thought the beggar was settled.' She eyed Steve. 'What now, damn it?'

'Find the seats.' He winked broadly. 'I'll send the brute packing.'

He went outside with the farm dog. They stopped at the fire door. 'Just wait there, Zac, I'll fetch you.' Steve returned to the foyer. Inside, the house-lights had dimmed and he opened the exit. Zac slipped in, his tail wagging.

Di giggled. 'He'll howl, Steve.'

'He'll sleep.'

'Then he'll snore!'

She was right, Zac's snores boomed, at their height in the love scene, and Di wept with laughter. When the film broke, he barked. The girl sobbed. 'Stop the beggar – do something, Steve, stop him!'

'He's *your* dog.'

'I'll not own him,' Di hooted. 'I bet he's here when he's missing – I bet he comes to the pictures!' She wiped her eyes. 'He goes *somewhere*.'

'Got a second home,' Steve said.

'No, he comes back neglected. Besides,' mused Di, 'there's Sal Wilson. She's got fanciful notions but I don't think she'd lie. Sal's seen Zac on the bog trail. Who lives in *that* region?'

A cheer rose; the screen flickered. 'Ah,' breathed Steve, his voice ghoulish, 'he's a Jekyll and Hyde dog!'

They slipped out at the curtain. Zac was grey in the starshine, and searchlights were probing. For a moment the dog turned, eyes like ice, then a plane throbbed. 'Is it one of ours?' Di said.

'There's no gunfire.'

Steve adjusted the bike lamps. The black hoods almost masked them, the glow a mere sliver. 'Where's Zac?' the girl asked him.

Steve said, 'Watch where you're going. Don't worry, I see him.'

Between the hedgerows, Zac ghosted.

The lane was dark where trees clustered, but the mongrel's

coat was even darker.

Now, the searchlights were swinging, shafting upwards at random, and Steve said, 'Bright beggars! If they catch you, you've had it.' He sensed Di's pang and backtracked. 'Not that *we* fly nights often. More likely out boozing.'

Zac had run ahead, growling. 'Fox,' said Steve, 'or a badger.' The ancient bike rattled.

'Steve . . .' The girl had dismounted where the lane became hilly. 'Be careful,' she pleaded. 'We'll miss you – *I'll* miss you.'

'You could marry me,' Steve said.

She stared at the searchlights. Neither spoke as they rested then she answered, voice husky, 'You could ask me again, Steve.'

'And again . . .'

'You'll be back.'

'Like the dog,' he assured her.

The bull was watered by bucket, penned up since Tuck's illness. Zac hurled scorn at the monster. His voice rose near the loose-box. He always swore as he passed and the bull, incensed, snorted. At last, the beast roused to fury, Zac quit the yard bristling.

Now, he marched to the meadows. Out of sight of the shorthorn, he flattened his hackles. The wind had turned, growing cooler, and lapwings were flocking, their whirling flight restless. A field gate was open. Through it, Zac saw the ponies.

The rough steeds had their heads down. As they scoffed Tuck's late grazing, the mongrel growled and they paused. The cobby skewbald surveyed him.

Zac remembered the skewbald, for its kick had been painful. Slowly, the dog moved towards them, at first crouching, his ears flat, then increasing his tempo. This time, he was cautious, avoiding their fetlocks. Eyes darting, he drove them, his neck stretched, tail flicking.

On the lane, their hooves clattered and Di, by the buildings, glanced at Jim, who had heard them. The ponies were pounding. Surprised, the girl watched them looming. 'Turn them, Jim,' she commanded. 'Wheel them into the midden; we'll see where they come from.'

'From the pasture,' he told her. He stopped their flight, arms extended. 'I saw them there,' the boy shouted. 'Shut the gate, miss, we got them!'

Zac came up, his tongue drooping, and Di eyed the compound. The ponies stood puffing.

'Whose are they, Jim, Wilsons'?'

'Aye,' the lad said, 'them's Wilsons'. I seen them at blacksmith's. It was Uncle who shod them.'

'Same lark,' the girl brooded. 'They'll claim they strayed from the hutment.' She stroked Zac, her mood gloomy. Steve had gone; she felt lonely. The thought of winter depressed her, months with only his letters. Many things made her dismal. Jim worked hard but lacked skills. The lad could not lay a hedge, far less work a plough team and Tuck was still convalescent.

The jobs grew like thistles, like the weeds in the turnips. Rose spent most days outdoors now, helping Di with the fieldwork. Their worries went deeper. Di feared for Steve's safety. More used to Roy's absence, her dread turned on aircraft, wrecked machines strewn in forests.

'Jim, we'll hang on to this lot.'

'To the nags?' He looked puzzled.

'To the nags. Toss some hay in. I'm sick of the Wilsons.' She knew her voice grated. 'Don't you give them those ponies; they'll see *me* first, is that clear? They'll see me if they want them. *I'll* lay down the terms, Jim.'

Three men came for the creatures: three lean, raw-jowled tinkers, led by Luke from the thresher. They were sullen, impassive, with a curious stillness. Di, confronted, was startled. 'Didn't hear you,' she told them. She had turned from the yard pump. 'Well,' she rapped, 'what do *you* want?'

'We've come for them, lady.'

They turned their eyes to the midden and Di said, 'You've lingered; I've had them three days here.'

'We looked all over,' Luke answered.

'Come on, I'm not stupid.'

They regarded her dumbly. The still faces were blank, chiselled bare of emotion. There was no trace of a gesture. She ran her gaze from their caps down to black, thin-soled shoes. Their apparel was sleazy. 'All over,' Luke echoed.

'You're a liar; you left them.'

'No, missy, they wandered.'

Luke's truculence glinted, an unspoken resentment. It chilled the girl, somehow threatening, and she wished Jim was with her. 'Well, they're *here*,' she said fiercely, with more spunk than she felt, 'and you'll pay to remove them. That's three days' hay and the grazing ...'

'We'll just take them and go, miss.'

Luke Wilson edged forward. He seemed to move like a zombie, the others beside him, hands in pockets. Di coloured. They knew Tuck was still weak and their insolence maddened her. She placed her back to the compound. 'Keep away,' she said quietly.

The men paused, their eyes shifty.

'Keep away. Don't you dare ...'

'They're ours,' Luke said. He took a half-pace and halted. The growl behind him was throaty. Di almost laughed her relief, for the three were transfigured. 'Call him off ...' They were shaking. 'Name of Christ, no harm, lady ...' Zac flanked them, lip curling. 'Call him off, we've touched nothing!'

'Down, Zac.'

'The dog's evil!'

'You reckon?' She let them quake for a moment. 'We were saying,' she mused, 'there's a matter of payment.'

'We'll be off.'

'Zac ...'

They dithered. 'We can't pay,' Luke said quickly.

'Suppose' – it was an idea from nowhere – 'suppose *I* pay,' Di suggested. They regarded her blankly. 'You can hedge and hoe, can't you? And *I'm* looking for labour. I'll make a deal on the ponies. You do my hedges and turnips – I'll pay you for working and hand the nags over. Of course, I'll dock for the fodder.'

'Be fair ...'

'Zac!'

'We'll do it.'

They did. She had seen better efforts but at least things were tidy. You could not ask for perfection. 'There's a war on,' Jim told her. He grinned and she cuffed him.

4

The rain scudded. It whipped trees where rooks huddled and swept in gusts across ploughland to spit in Tuck's wood-fire. He had made a blaze by the sheep-fold, breaking up an old hurdle. He rubbed his hands. His face tingled.

He was back in the weather. Chisel-headed irons heated, the block and tarpot set near them. 'Get a move on, Shep, damn you.'

The shepherd loomed slowly. His pace seldom varied, the shuffling plod of a lifetime, much of it spent on Tuck's acres. 'And damn *you*,' said the shepherd. The man earned his shillings – in mud, drought and snowdrift. 'You weren't so lively a while back.'

'B'God,' Tuck said, 'time's money.' He considered the other, the sunken head, hollow-featured; the armour of sacking. Shep would die at his own pace – knowing best, sly, cantankerous. 'There's no profit at this rate.'

'I can pack my bag, master.'

'To go where?'

'Where skill's valued.'

'Good riddance!'

'Or *retire*. Time I rested.'

Tuck grunted. He said, eyeing the sheep pen, the fat lambs with black noses, 'It's the sheep keeps you going.' Tuck inhaled the smell of them. Their breath mingled with woodsmoke, sweetly pungent and steamy. 'Without sheep, you'd be buried.' He grasped his knife and a whetstone.

The old man caught a lamb and hauled the mettled beast forward. 'It's all gone,' he reflected, 'time when good men meant something. No respect for us nowadays – damned chits giving orders.'

'Don't you let my girl hear you!'

'I'd tell her straight, master.' Shep turned the sheep on its back, watching Tuck slit the scrotum. 'Whoa, my son; whoa, you varmint! Time that girl o' yours settled and made a home like her mother. Chits of girls up on tractors; waltzing round wearing trousers! War's demented the women.'

'They got *you* working, you beggar.'

'Whoa!' croaked Shep.

'Hold him still.' It was late to be gelding and the lambs had grown powerful. 'Hold him still, man, we'll tail him.' The tails of sheep harboured pests. Tuck drew an iron from the embers. He said, 'They got *you* out stooking, you and him from the dairy. That's more than *I've* managed.'

'World's gone mad,' Shep protested. 'Blamed women a-farming!'

Tuck toiled without speaking. Setting chisel to flesh, he pressed down against the block. The wool scorched. Amid smoke, the tail parted and Tuck tarred the stump. Shep said, 'Farming's a man's job; us could do with your lad here. Young Roy understands.'

'He'll be here.' Crouched by the flames, Tuck looked thoughtful. The released wether bleated. It wandered off and he muttered, 'He'll be here when the war's done. You'll see – he'll be master.'

'I'll be gone,' Shep predicted. 'Last bugger near killed me; I'll not live out this 'un.'

'He'll take up a good farm, Shep.' The rain dripped from Tuck's cap. He said, 'In good heart and fettle,' and, as the next sheep was tumbled, 'I'll see Roy starts aright – I'll make damned sure of that much.'

'Maybe ...'

'I'll make certain.'

'You near didn't, I reckon. You want to watch this rain, master. You nearly left us wi' women, nought but women for gaffers. You'll not want no setbacks.'

'There'll be no setbacks,' Tuck promised. He walked the farm with Zac later, glad the gelding was over. He felt fit, damn the weather! Rose had said, 'You're a madman. Get wet, it's your lookout. You'll be back where you were, Wilf.'

But the ploughing was urgent. Di could not get the seed in.

By the warren, he paused. The rain had eased to a drizzle and the fire, almost dead, trickled smoke into greyness. He could hear Shep's rough cough and, when the man's bitch ran forward, the farmer rebuffed her. She had followed the mongrel. 'Get you back!'

He called Zac. They went on, Tuck observing, 'Don't you heed *her*, she's flighty.' A soggy pheasant rose steeply. Its wings whirred for a moment then froze, and the bird glided. 'There's a lot to be done, dog.' Tuck's gaze roamed. 'We'll be busy.'

Tuck rested, his eyes distant. He had had time for thinking. They could use a new tractor. Roy would want modern tools and Tuck had thumbed the farm weeklies. He stretched broad bed-sore shoulders while Zac sat beside him. Aloud, the man mused, 'A Fergy – something useful for roadwork.'

It would pay him, he reckoned. True, the outlay was daunting but the prospects inveigled. He could make up time faster, adapt wagons for hauling, maybe sell the old Morris. Jim could drive a light tractor. The Case was a beggar; she took a man's handling. The new ones were simple. Jim would cope, given teaching.

'Come on, Zac.' The dog bounded.

They went down by the bomb-pits, crossing wet, greasy acres where land-drains were running. The craters were ugly. Filled now with brown water, they simmered like cauldrons. Tuck spat, stepping round them. It was time they were filled in, but he knew he could not hire a bulldozer. They were all out on war work.

'Tuck!' The back door was open. He could see Rose was flustered.

'Aye, I'm damp,' he admitted.

'Yes.' She took it too lightly. 'You must change.' No reprovals. He picked up the yard brush and cleaned his boots, glancing sideways. There was no mention of Benson, no doom-laden sermon. He looked up, growing worried.

'It's Roy . . .'

His gut tightened. All day the boy had been with him – in thought, in Tuck's scheming. He might have known it meant something.

'He's written.' She was flushed with excitement. 'He'll be with us for Christmas. He's got a week, same as Steve, and it's settled for Christmas. We'll be together,' Rose told him.

Jim lifted the harrow and kicked off the rubbish. Twitching the lines, he urged the mare to the headland, swung her round and trudged forward. Boy and horse plodded slowly, raking up the dead couch-grass the frost had whitened.

There had been several frosts. At his uncle's, where he lodged, they had killed the caterpillars on Rutter's cabbages. The air was bitter. It came, Jim's aunt said, from Russia, from a tank-threatened Moscow. He did not know. Jim only knew that his eyes wept.

At dawn, cycling from Murton full of the tea Aunt Flo brewed him, his ears would freeze, his hands perish. He would cry at the torment. Yet Jim was proud of his farm job and Tuck, whom he reverenced. 'Whoa!' He blew on his fingers. Again cleaning the tines, he clucked at the dobbin, then went on harrowing.

The clouds chilled and the sky was arctic. A field away, Tuck was drilling. His pair of horses moved briskly, the man behind them swift-striding, from time to time stepping on to the seed drill to check the container. As it emptied, he replenished, shooting sacks from a wagon.

Jim was envious. The strength and skills of the farmer filled the lad with ambition. He would not, he had told Flo, always drive the old dobbin.

'Poor Jim.' She had eyed Rutter. 'As well the Lord gave him *sinew*.'

But there were hints of fulfilment, for Tuck had mentioned the tractor and now, as the air sliced, the lad imagined the power, his hands on the throttle – and telling the others. 'Gid-up, mare!' On they shambled. He would learn, the boy reckoned; soon pick up the wrinkles.

'Hey, you daft bloody mongrel!'

Zac ran up, pleased to find him, and Jim beamed a greeting. He was fond of the dog. The two would sometimes go ratting, Jim collecting the rat tails, which earned him a bounty: sixpence a half-dozen. He kept them in bundles, looped with string, neat as banknotes. 'Heck, Zac, it's a cold 'un!'

He thought of Zac and the ponies. '*Tinkers, Zac!*' he teased, grinning. Zac growled and he chuckled. Catch Jim scared of a farm dog! He smirked, walking taller. 'Superstition!' he muttered. You might have doubts about screechowls and ravens on rooftops, but Zac – gentle Jesus!

Di arrived with the nosebags. 'Stand the mare in the lee, Jim, let her feed in the shelter.' He admired Wilf Tuck's daughter. Her face was blue but still handsome and he knew why Steve wooed her, as Flo Rutter put it. Flo's interest was beady, like a bird's sharp surveillance. 'She's not decided, I notice; there's no ring on her finger.' To which Rutter had answered, 'More's the sense, I do reckon. Why wed to be widowed?'

Now Di said, 'You need warming.' She took the top off a Thermos. 'Hot soup ...'

Jim was grateful. His own girl, when he got one, would be like Miss Di, for she made you feel someone just to be along with her. 'Heard from Steve?' he asked gravely. He might himself join the Air Force, thought Jim, when he was older. Or, like Roy, the Commandos.

'Steve's on ops,' the girl told him.

'That'll be over France.'

'I don't know.'

The lad nodded. Gulping soup, he said wisely, 'Careless talk ...'

'Yes,' the girl said, an ear turned. She was trying to listen but the mare shook her nosebag and, 'Hush!' Di exhorted. 'Damn the horse, now I've lost it. Could have been a van passing. Have you heard the raid warning?'

'Out here?' Jim looked doubtful. 'East wind?'

'Aye.' She shivered. 'I just thought – *there!* It's distant.'

Jim listened. 'It's *summat* ...' He tucked his thumbs in his

95

waistcoat. It was an old one of Rutter's. 'A plane,' he said slowly. 'She'll be low, I do reckon.'

The dog cowered. 'Zac can't stand them.' Di stooped to the mongrel. She smoothed his ruff. 'Not the low ones.'

'Nor my auntie's cat,' Jim said. 'It's the din. They be deafened.'

The wind numbed the girl's temples. She straightened, her hair blowing. Searching the view, she demanded, 'Can you spot it? Is it coming this way, Jim?'

'Dunno ...' He held the mare, squinting. A dark dot was expanding, winging under the cloud-base, almost clipping the woodlands. Rooks were rising from treetops. Tuck had drawn in his horses and clung to their bridles. 'Aye,' gulped Jim, 'she's a-coming, nigh ploughing a furrow!'

The mongrel had scooted. Racing over the field, the dog made for Tuck's wagon, reached the wheels and dived under. Prone, Zac started to tremble. He knew that thunder of engines and still dreamed the nightmare.

The roar had drubbed, growing louder, the plane plunging lower. Then an engine was flaming, tongues of fire trailing from it, fragmenting and glowing, each breath incandescent. Parts had sheered from the aircraft, spinning into the darkness. It had sped like a train. Sparks had gushed and fumes billowed. As it ran out of airspace, the doomed craft had juddered, contorted on impact, then brushed on, its wings broken.

Dead couch drifted. The wind balled the thin grass roots, rolling them in white bundles, like ghosts on the tilt, as the thunder came closer.

Di said, 'Is it a German?'

'Beggared if I can place her.'

'God, it's low!'

'She's a bomber ...' Jim stared over the hedge. He could make out two engines but, head-on, no markings. 'By chance, she'll pass by the buildings.'

The mare had her head up. Di could see Tuck's steeds fretting, her dad's rumbustious anger, but his curses were smothered. The motors drowned comment. Flocks of pigeons rose swiftly. Full of kale, they fled west, the machine booming past them.

'Damme,' Jim bawled, eyes sparkling, 'I'm blamed if that's not a Blenheim!' The plane had veered into profile. As it shot over the farm buildings, a propeller-boss glinted and Di glimpsed the roundels. Her heart jumped.

'You *certain*?'

'No mistake – she's a Blenheim.'

'Jim, the plane's not in trouble?'

He grinned. 'Watch her bustle!' The craft was rising, less raucous, its banking climb graceful. 'Nay,' the lad declared sagely, 'yon's true as a swallow.'

'Mad fools!' Tuck was fuming. 'Putting fear in young horses!' His voice carried across the field now but Di took no interest. She was trembling, her gaze lofted. '*One* lot home,' Jim said stoutly. 'Miss Di, you look frozen.'

She shrugged. 'Stood here gawping ...'

'Fair shaking,' the boy said. 'You and Zac – both a-tremble.'

5

Ice patterned the windows and Tuck, in for breakfast, sat close to the hearth while the girl read Steve's letter. 'He's been made a flight-sergeant.' She peered at the rambling scrawl.

She smiled, her tea cooling.

Rose brought Tuck eggs on toast and the women swopped glances. 'Well,' said Rose, 'that's promotion. I'm sure Steve deserves it. He'll get more pay now.'

'While things last,' Tuck said gruffly. 'The lad's got no future.'

'That's *nice*!' Rose admonished.

Di said, banging her cup down, 'Fine thanks for Steve's help, Dad!'

'Huh!' Her father ate briskly. 'Nothing wrong with him,' Tuck said. 'Like the boy. I'm just saying ...'

'We *know*, Tuck.'

'Looking for'ard.' In his daughter's best interests. The boy had no prospects.

'Opening your great mouth,' Rose told him. 'The lass isn't stupid.'

He was glad when Jim called, urging him to the dairy. Not that Tuck wanted problems but he could handle the cowman. Women's moods left him baffled. He went to the cowsheds.

The yard dung was frozen. Tuck ducked as he entered to avoid the fang-like icicles. They hung from eaves between old oaken doorposts buffed smooth four times daily by the broad flanks of milch cows. 'Well?' He eyed the herd keenly.

'You'd best look,' said the cowman, 'for I'm through with damned troubles.' He was hand-milking Brindle, his hunched frame contorted. The machine-milker was not new but some old cows still refused it. 'You'd best look and do summat. That machine's good for nothing.'

'Not the only one,' Tuck rasped. He stomped the line of tails, mumbling. They were Tuck's pride, his shorthorns. Blossom, Flower, Brindle's daughters – prize-winners, by thunder – by a bull they called dangerous! 'What's the gripe this time, damn it?'

'Cups aren't sucking.'

The pail frothed.

'Man, you're never done grousing!'

The cowman scraped his stool backwards. He winced, cranking upright, each vertebra racking. He looked grotesque in his white skull cap, puce with cold and from choler. 'Grousing, eh? I could grouse!' He held the pail, his back twisted. 'Ye'd grouse, milking this lot. Half won't take the machine on; t'other half, it falls off them! I'm past needing the trouble.'

'You're spoiled,' said the farmer. 'There's no pleasing you, cowman. Drove me daft for that machine and you can't breathe but cuss it! You've not stopped since we got it.'

'For it's never been right.'

'Never been rightly handled!'

The ground was well trodden. '*You* handle the beggar!' The same damned futile skirmish – it slogged on like trench warfare.

'I've no time to stand wrangling.'

'Nor I to cart mangolds. By chance, she's froze, bitch contraption! I'll not go wi'out breakfast; *you* feed them this morning.'

Tuck fumed to the stable. Loading shovel and pitchfork, he drove to the root pile. Cold, the horse jogged for warmth and he grasped the reins numbly, hell-damning his fortune. The men he wanted sent letters; the men he paid were decrepit. They should be in the churchyard, his cowman and shepherd.

At the mound, he alighted. Chucking his coat on the horse, Tuck set to with the shovel. The soil casing was frosted. He glowed as he breached it, his work making him hot, then cleared the straw lining. Well preserved, the roots cheered him. They looked good: firm and florid.

Now he used the pitchfork. With each jab of the prongs, he took two heavy mangolds and tossed them adroitly. They banged on the cart boards. For a while, he worked smoothly: jab, hoist, a deft flick. The trick was not to impale them so far that they stuck there.

As the cart filled, Di joined him. 'I'll drive,' she said simply.

'Right.' They stopped on the pasture and Tuck dropped the tailboard. 'Get on steady,' he grunted. The roots started falling. She drove while he shovelled. 'About Steve . . .' They spread a wake of red mangolds. '. . . don't mistake me,' Tuck told her.

'Stop worrying,' Di said.

'All I meant – well, air-gunner, it isn't a trade, lass.' The iron ground made the cart jolt. 'I'm thinking of *you*, Di.'

The dog brought the herd down. Zac needed no supervision, briskly stirring the loafers, alert as he hustled. By and by, when the cattle were munching, he jumped up with the farmer. Tuck shot the last roots.

'Mind,' he wheezed, 'Steve's a good 'un; his old job'll be waiting.' He eyed the bold-patterned beasts tucking in to the mangolds. 'But that's no proper future for a daughter of mine, girl.'

'Dad, forget it.'

'Not a future with prospects.'

The girl turned the cart-horse. 'Who has?' she demanded. 'Dear God, the way things are going; no help in the offing . . .'

'I don't know – now I'm fit. There's a lot to make up but I'll get my back to it. Soon have the farm shipshape.'

She sighed, the horse quickening. Bloody farm! Her chin lifted. 'That's not what I meant, Dad.'

Zac made for the gunsite. The lane's verges were brittle, stiff as the hazel which flanked them, its wands glistening. Zac scurried. On the rime, his pads whispered, a faint click coming from his claws as he hogged the road's centre.

It was quiet. A small convoy of lorries, their radiators muffled, crossed the heath, driven by soldiers. He let them wait. A horn blared. At length, the dog condescended and they passed into the whiteness, their tracks black on the hoar-frost.

The gun stood up bleakly. By the frozen emplacement, a brazier beckoned, its heat like a mirage. Huddled round in their greatcoats, the crew watched Zac join them. 'Time off?' they puffed, stamping. 'Back again, you skiving mongrel!' They wore brown Balaclavas and held mugs in their mittens, one tossing a biscuit.

Zac basked in the warmth. He often called at the outpost, assured of a welcome. He liked the banter and tidbits. 'Bloody hell,' said a corporal, 'you're not back to the jungle?' The man scanned the timbers. 'Not in *this*!' His teeth chattered.

Their camaraderie pleased; it struck a chord in the mongrel. He watched one then another. 'Want to bet?' asked a soldier. 'Ten bob to a Woodbine he'll go for the forest.'

'What's the bloody attraction?'

'Dogs and trees – well known fact, corp.'

They tipped their mugs. Zac was aware of their interest, that they liked the diversion. His nose was damp, his ears forward. 'Smart dog,' said the corporal. 'Knows a thing or two we don't.'

'No one tells *us* sod all, corp!'

'Hey-up, lads, look at that lot ...' They turned to the hutment. The three Wilsons were leaving, striking over the heathland, outlined on the frostscape. Zac jumped up on the sandbags. Luke was leading the trio, his steps taking him towards Murton. 'Look at him in the leather!' The flying-jacket was bulky. Luke was lost in its collar. 'Fur-lined,' said a soldier.

'It wasn't won in a raffle.'

'Time *we* looked in the woods, corp; there's maybe a sale on!'

'Bloody ghouls,' said the corporal. He drained his mug. 'Right, let's have you ...'

The dog dropped into the heather. The tinkers were distant. As the gun crew got busy, he loped to the dwellings.

Sal's thin fowls protested. They were hunched on the rubbish, their plumes fluffed for warmth; the hard ground was scratch-resistant. Zac examined the huts. There was no one about and the dog explored coldly where scrap and refuse lay frosted.

From the trees, a cry reached him. He stood still. Inclined to run, the dog nevertheless waited. He knew the voice of the child and the second call drew him. Near the wood's edge, he paused. The black timbers were hostile. Clawing up at the sky-wall, they haunted the mongrel. Zac listened. The scream urged him forward.

Barely into the forest, he came to the sheet-ice. Overhung by chill branches, it had set on a hollow which held stagnant water, a grey winter casing that creaked as Sal dithered. The woman was frantic. Frozen reeds met the mongrel – and, beyond, was the toddler, a petrified bundle far out from the fringe, mesmerized by Sal's shrieks and the sound of ice cracking.

'*Holy Mother of Jesus* ...' Sal's prayer was a whimper.

She stepped back, her eyes rolling. Her weight had fractured the ice-case, its noise like a gunshot. Casting round, she ran wailing. A fallen birch pole was handy and, fretting, she tugged it. The frost held it anchored.

Zac had moved to the reed bed. Her face rigid, Sal watched him, heard the crisp platform moaning. She saw him stop, forepaws skidding. His snout hit the ice. Scrambling up, Zac worked forward, better balanced, his legs splayed.

It was a slow, jerky process. With each creak, the dog paused. But his glare was determined, set fast on the child, whose pale features stared back, gradually becoming nearer.

'Holy Mary,' Sal pleaded.

She closed her eyes, almost fainting. There was a snap: more ice breaking. It seemed to run through the hollow, the frozen sump rumbling, and she forced her lids open.

The boy was flat on his chest. One arm was outstretched, the hand fused to Zac's collar, its grip choking the mongrel. Ice was opening around them. Paws scrabbling, Zac strained.

Very slowly, they shifted, as he hauled the frightened child sled-like.

It seemed to Sal never-ending.

In his battle for purchase, Zac would fall and lie kicking. Clawing up, he strove on, sometimes labouring crabwise, his weight deployed sideways; other times, pulling forward, head down, his tongue lolling. Sal could see trapped air spreading, undermining the platform. Then, again, she was running, making now for the reed bed, reaching out as they neared it.

The whole ice-case was heaving.

Wildly, Sal snatched her son and, shaking violently, hugged him. Zac had slumped on the bank. At first, the child merely quivered then, his shock dissipating, began to bawl like a weanling, and was whirled home by the woman.

Panting, Zac jogged behind them. Once, Sal turned and looked back, but sped on without stopping. Concerned, the dog followed. He heard the door of the hut slam. Puzzled, Zac sat outside, gazing up at the handle.

For some minutes, he waited as the child's noise abated then the door was eased open. A small face shone with warmth. 'Damn'ee,' Sal exclaimed, 'shut it!' She peered out for a moment. It was as if she were struggling, her emotions in conflict as the door closed, banishing Zac.

He lay about looking hopeful. There were eyes at a window but the filth on it dulled them. At last, his patience expended, the dog mooched off through the hutment, his manner dejected, tail pendulous.

Zac went back to the Bofors. It stood up in a whiteness that avalanched earthwards, erasing the landline, merging heath with the heavens. Specks of snow drifted past him. 'Had enough?' called a soldier.

'Get along,' urged another.

At the sheep folds, he snuffled. Both herders were working, no bitch to console him. Nor was Tuck's growl a comfort. 'Stand back, you'll not help, dog.' The man cranked the tractor. It backfired, handle kicking, and he clutched a thumb, swearing. 'Bloody cow ...'

103

Tuck looked evil. 'She'd break my arm if she could. Bloody Case,' he exploded, 'one damned frost and she's vicious.' He eyed the dog. 'What's *your* trouble? You've no cause to be sulking, it's me the brute's clobbered!'

6

Nearing Christmas, Tuck and Rose drove to Ringwood. It was an annual event, she to shop, he to market, and Zac travelled with them. Beside the lanes, steers stared glumly, their pastures frost-blighted. The cold had left the grass limp and the beasts looked for rations.

Rose gazed from the Morris. Stark elms trooped on hummocks and smoke plumed the hamlets. At that season, ivy leaves greened the waysides, giving shelter to sparrows which fled the truck's rampage. Rose shared their fluster. 'Slow down, Tuck, or you'll kill us!'

He obeyed with reluctance and she tugged her coat round her. The cab was draughty; its seat, bruising. At each pothole she winced, clutching Zac as they cornered and the ill-sprung truck lurched. 'I don't know why I do this.' She scowled at the driver. 'It's not travelling, it's torment.'

'She's no slouch,' Tuck responded. He revved and Rose grumbled. Farther on, folds held wethers, fat and fit now for grading. 'Shep's look better,' he boasted.

Rose said, 'Damn the sheep, Wilfred, I'm sick of this lorry. Other people have cars. It's about time that we did.'

'Cars?' He eyed his wife sideways.

'Watch the road!'

'A *car*?' Tuck said. They charged on through a village whose grey-shingled church spire was streaked with bird-droppings. Jackdaws circled it, clacking. 'What use would a car be?'

'We'd travel in comfort.'

'There's buses for comfort.'

'Precious few,' his wife told him. 'I'd like a car, Tuck, we've earned it.' She smiled tightly at Zac, as though the matter was settled.

She watched the lane twist and burrow. Holly trees flicked

105

the window, their lower leaves prickly, the pale high ones smoother. She must soon get some sprigs cut. She would make the house festive, especially the parlour, before Roy's arrival.

'We've no money for cars, Rose.'

'There's enough for a small one. We're not impoverished,' Rose snapped.

'Rainy days . . .' He looked shifty.

Tuck changed gear, his thumb still aching. The reminder was timely. He had his own plan of purchase, the notion was still guarded, undisclosed to the woman. 'By and by,' the man mumbled, 'we need things on the farm first – investments, replacements.'

'So you *always* say, Wilfred.'

She eyed her list: tea, flour, spices. Jumbled roofs rose outside and she told him, 'Damned lorry! Drop me here by the shops, I'll be glad to be walking. It's not fit to be driven.'

She glowered as the truck disappeared, Zac's head poking from it. Then, her chagrin forgotten, Rose pitched into the bustle which lapped from the market round the pubs, stalls and chandlers. She meant, whatever the war news, to make Christmas successful.

Old men grinned, their breath beery; harassed wives took a tipple. There was a seasonal temper, a glint from the natives that defied the year's tidings. They had hoarded their coupons, saved to buy food and presents.

Rose had grown up among them. 'How's Roy?' they asked, stopping: chawbacon farmers and smiths' wives. And Rose, her bag filling, said he was coming for Christmas and she must get on, for the shop queues were growing.

Some, like Flo, were persistent. 'My sister's boy's on the convoys. He says the sinking is dreadful; folk don't know. All that drowning. Those U-boats are wicked. Everything will get scarcer.'

'I daresay.'

'And poor Dinah – her so bright – she'll miss London. There's no life for a girl here; bored stiff, I do reckon.'

'Di's doing her bit, Flo.'

Rutter's beaky wife squinted. 'Not engaged yet, I notice; nor much chance out in Murton, with the young men enlisted. Mind, there's Steve ...'

Rose escaped her. Hustling on, she met others, men and women with sons gone, daughters travelling to factories. Most she knew as if cousins, folk racy of the soil, hard to move, stubborn people. Stony ground for dictators, she thought pugnaciously.

Her bag was heavy. As she made for the market in search of the Morris, she spotted the mongrel. 'Where's Tuck?' she said. 'Find him.' It posed Zac no problem, for he had come from the tractors. Tuck was still with the salesman.

'I'm weighed down, Tuck,' she told him.

'Rest yourself,' said the salesman. 'Save your strength for the cooking!'

'That's the least of it,' Rose said, 'there's plenty else waiting.' Three dozen fowls to be plucked, eggs to scrub, plus the feeding. 'I can't stand here talking.'

'How d'you like this one, missus?' Tuck's fist thumped the Fergy and Rose eyed it vaguely. It made the Case seem a relic; its lines were light and slender, the paintwork dove-coloured. Zac was sniffing the tyres.

'Come on, Wilf ...'

'Reconditioned.' He pushed his cap back, his face boyish. 'Near as new – she's a greyhound!'

'And she pulls,' said the salesman. 'Cheap to run and does most things. She'll turn on a sixpence. That's the new type of tractor. Every farmer will have one.'

'Aye,' said Rose, 'in his pipe-dreams.'

Tuck beamed. 'She's no pipe-dream.'

'You're not thinking ...' Her eyes flashed. She knew the expression, his grin of confusion. 'Lord,' she re-phrased the question, 'don't tell me ...'

'I've bought her.'

'With what?'

He looked sheepish. Rose seethed. Provoked, she rasped, 'The car, Wilfred?' Tuck had spent the car money! Someone ran from an office and a voice inquired, 'Where's Pearl

107

Harbour?' She was still flushed with anger. 'The Japs have bombed the Yank fleet there. On the news ...'

There was silence, an uncanny hiatus. They were grouped by the market, car and tractor now forgotten. Tuck's wife gripped his elbow. Knots of men stood together, their heads close, and she asked, 'What's it mean; what will happen?'

'Seems we're *all* in it now, girl.'

'The same boat, Mrs Tuck.'

'The Americans?' Rose said. 'They'll be coming?'

'Like before,' mused the salesman.

'Thank God,' she breathed slowly, as if a dark night had lightened. 'I don't mean for the bombing; for hope at last.' For a glimmer.

Jim went into the stable. The horses called and he fussed them. At each stall, he talked softly, his breath mingling with their breath. He had some corn in a pocket and gave the grains to the creatures. Their twitching noses amused him, the gentle eagerness for such slight rewards.

The youth liked their kindness. His uncle often told horse tales. Once, according to Rutter, a plough-team from Murton, let out to take water, had met a babe in the pathway. The mite had crawled from a nearby cottage.

'Damned,' he said, 'if those toilers, each nigh on a ton-weight, didn't pick their damned feet up like blamed ballerinas and hop over that infant, never touching it.'

Jim believed him. He stopped at Tuck's shelf of medicines. In one tin was black treacle, used to tempt the poor feeders. The lad dipped a finger. 'Still hungry?' Di Tuck said.

He turned, startled.

'You didn't need to come in, Jim.' It was Boxing Day morning. She looked glum. 'The boss told you.'

'Aye, but ...' Jim sucked the finger.

Di shrugged. 'We're all gloomy.'

'Your brother's leave being cancelled?'

'Didn't help.' And Steve flying, she thought.

'After all the preparing.' Jim frowned, looking troubled.

'That was cruel on the missus. All her bustling and chasing. Your ma was excited.'

'We all were.'

And the day was a let-down. They had tended the bullocks, tossing out kale and oat-straw, then tried to be cheerful, to match the spruced parlour. Rose had strung it with cards and put up fir and holly, and Tuck had brought in a Yule log. But Roy's absence pervaded.

'Bloody flop,' Di related, her hands on a pitchfork. 'Bloody worrying, too, Jim.'

No lift in the sherry, no fun in the basting. The empty seat had mocked dinner and dulled the edge of their relish. Only Zac had been happy, allowed extra helpings. Even he had looked baleful when the washing-up was finished.

'It's not knowing,' Di grunted. She refilled the iron hayracks. 'To stop his leave – I don't like it.'

Jim sniffed. 'Summat's happening.'

'Bloody fine, Jim, at Christmas!'

Rose, she thought, had coped bravely. Just the once had she vanished, reappearing soon red-eyed but scornful of fuss, though Tuck's arm consoled her. At church, Rose had prayed quietly on her knees for several minutes.

Jim said now, 'We'll be hearing. Full o' tricks, the Commandos.'

'I hope to God he'll be careful.'

Rutter's nephew looked doubtful. It seemed an odd sort of word, the way he reckoned things happening, but he did not dispute it. 'He's still got his leave owing.' Jim could see she was anguished.

'I wish he'd never gone off, Jim.' Di paused. 'Him *or* Steve.'

'They'd to go.'

'Had they hell.'

'*I'll* be going.'

'You?' She scowled, and rested the fork. 'You grow up first,' Di muttered, remorseful next instant, for his face plunged a fathom. 'Wait and see, Jim, we need you. You're important.'

He blushed. 'I dunno . . .'

'Wait till the tractor's delivered!'

She smiled at his pleasure. Christmas, too, had had moments – taking gifts to the cowman, his glare almost genial; and to the shepherd. Then they had toured the farm creatures.

That was Tuck's special ritual: extra corn for the horses, scraps and milk for the pigs, tidbits for the mousers. For a while, Rose had brightened, watching Zac's look of pain as the cats munched their presents.

'Damn it,' Di told the farm lad, 'since you're here, don't go broody.' She heaved the fork to him. 'Come on, get that coat off.'

She leaned on the half-door. It was not much use fretting. In the draught, the girl shuddered. The wind was set for the Continent, blowing viciously.

The soldier raised his head slowly. A bullet hummed like a jack-snipe. He ducked behind the stacked boxes. 'Bloody hell!' his mate gritted. 'Buck up with that dressing.'

'Where's he shooting from, Tuck-o?'

''Cross the street, first floor window.' Roy had spotted the sniper.

'Come flaming cruising to Norway!'

'See the fjords and die happy . . .'

It was brisk as the gunshots, a quick fearful banter. The sky was cold, smoke-apparelled. A Bren fired in spasms. 'Should have been at home,' Roy said. He crouched by the fish crates.

Near him, the medics were stooping over the messily wounded sergeant. He looked, thought Roy, like a rabbit half-eaten by ferrets. 'Could have had tea in bed.' He watched the road. 'Walked the farm.'

'Farm? I'd settle for Shoreditch.'

They had sailed on Christmas Eve, putting into the Shetlands before making for Vaagsfjord. Planes had covered the raid. They had copped it, the Blenheims; Roy had seen two in trouble. Vaagso itself was a small town, now an enemy shore base. Huddled under a rockface, its wooden buildings burned fiercely in the main street, dumps and petrol exploding.

Roy had fought to the yard. There, pinned down by the sniper, he could see black fumes swirling, hear the dull thud of mortars. A dog jogged past, its cool indifference spooky.

'Got a dog on that farm, corp?'

'Aye.' The box by him splintered, the slug passing through it. He drew a bead on the window. The maw was dark, the foe hidden: Roy was forced to duck quickly. There was a snap in his pocket of his folk with the mongrel, Zac sitting up proudly. He glanced at the sergeant.

'Easy, sarge.'

The man gasped. He looked deathly. They had shot him with morphia and done their best with the dressing.

'Where's the R.A.P.?' Roy said.

'Down the Strand.' They leered grimly. The two medics were Cockneys. 'See you later, we'll stroll it!'

More bullets came swiftly.

'Not with him up there,' Roy said.

'Sod him, this one's not waiting.' They had wheeled up a handcart and bent to the sergeant. Humour drained, one said tersely, 'He needs help bloody quick, mate.'

'One minute,' Roy told them. 'Give me one and then shift him.' He squeezed out round the crates and they watched him run forward, head low, grenade fisted. Flaming debris was falling from buildings to the gutters. He reached the gate. Smoke concealed him.

Out to sea, ships were firing. A plane roared low, marked with crosses. The medics crouched by the handcart. Burning timbers cascaded and ahead, in the shambles, a muffled crump sounded. A grenade.

'Here we go, sarge!'

7

Rain drubbed the farmhouse.

'You all right?' asked the postman. She was aware he had waited. 'Yes,' said Rose. 'You'll drown, damn it.' She went to the parlour. Water streamed on the windows. She always went to the parlour – always had, Rose reflected, the hundred times in her mind she had lived through this moment.

She left the envelope sealed. In her mind, she had torn it and read the War Office statement, but the words were superfluous. She had no need to consult them; no more need than the postman. Instead, she took down the photo and pressed Roy's face to her.

Rose could hear the rain splashing. In a while, the dog whimpered. She met Zac's eyes as hers opened. His gaze mirrored her grief and, when she perched on the settle, his head found her apron. 'Aye, *you* know,' sighed the woman. Not, perhaps, what Rose Tuck knew but at least that she was shattered.

The girl found them together. She read the telegram dumbly. At last, she said, 'Oh my God, Ma.'

'Poor Tuck ...'

'It's not true, Ma.'

'It's the truth, girl,' Rose told her. 'I always thought it would happen.' She fought for strength, her heart stricken. Rose had the steel to surmount it; in time, to rivet the fissures, but Tuck lacked her armour. She said, 'It'll break him. He lived for Roy taking over; never doubted Roy's future.'

It rained for forty-eight hours.

Benson called, his coat dripping.

'Rose ...'

She nodded. 'We'll manage.'

'Wilf?' he asked, his voice doubtful.

112

Tuck kept working from habit but Roy's death brought a numbness, filled him with a darkness that frightened the women. He plumbed depths at that moment untouched in his illness. Then, a spark had persisted; now, his eyes did not flicker. He spoke in grunts, the tone chilling.

'Turn it off, woman, damn you.'

The radio crackled. Outside, thunder was rumbling, upsetting the programme. It was a broadcast on Vaagso, describing the raid there. The damage done was recited: to stores, barracks, factories. 'Commando losses were slight.'

'Switch it off; turn the lies off.'

When they sent Roy's possessions, Tuck refused to go through them and take the lighter or penknife. The few things filled a shoebox. 'There's a letter,' his wife said. She paused, her eyes stinging. 'From his unit commander. Read it, Wilf, you'll be proud ...'

'Letter?'

'Read it.'

'They've left the boy lying dead and we've got a damned letter? I *was* proud of him, woman – proud of Roy on the farm. What do *they* know?'

'Tuck,' she pleaded.

'With their slight bloody losses.'

'Stop it, Tuck!' Rose was shaking. 'It's the service tomorrow. Think of Di ...'

'It's no good, Rose.'

'It *must* be.' Her fists clenched. 'We've got to face it together. You've got to pull through, Tuck.'

Rain spattered the churchyard. Zac, left at the lych-gate, watched them haul up the lane, those damp figures from Murton, the hard grey light on them. They looked strange in stiff collars, men like Shep and the cowman, young Jim and the blacksmith. Women passed in small clusters, heads down in the weather.

When they were all inside, the dog shifted. At the church door, he listened, their husky tones muffled. It was dry in the porch and he lay on the slabs there. Papers, pinned to a board, contained notes for the parish: a list of Air Raid Precautions, the rota for wardens. Outside, damp tombs glistened.

Head on paws, the dog waited. A truck squelched through the village. For a moment, his lip twitched, but his challenge was abortive and the truck passed.

Tuck was first from the service. He came out like a bull, shoulders hunched, lunging forward. Others paused; he did not. Ignoring the downpour, he thrust on, striding wildly, his open coat flying.

'Dad ...' The voice died behind him.

Rose halted her daughter. 'Let him go; you won't stop him.'

Di bent to the mongrel. 'Oh, Zac!'

Tuck had vanished.

'Come on home,' Rose said quietly.

'I've the car,' said Doc Benson. He concealed the flask from them. 'Let him walk. Give him time, Rose.'

Tuck lurched through the rainstorm, climbing over wet ploughland, his best boots mud-smothered. The brown leather was fouled. It had always been glassy, Tuck proud of the polish. Now, the heavy soil balled as he wrenched his feet through it.

Dense with cloud, the sky darkened, shedding curtains of vapour along the ridge to which he staggered. At the craters Tuck stopped and looked into the dark water. He was drenched, his clothes shapeless, the clay thick on his trousers.

Obscene, the pits mocked him. They desecrated Tuck's acres – 'Roy's acres!' he bellowed. 'God!' he moaned, scooping soil, clutching it as he straightened. He hurled the earth at the bomb-hole. Its belch echoed upwards.

'Christ!' Tuck's fury was savage. 'Not so much as a body!' He scooped again, on his knees now. 'Couldn't spare us that little – his body to bury!' He hurled the clod downwards. 'God's damned mercy!' he shouted. He flung the earth, his voice breaking. Again, the farmer's fists scrabbled.

Again, the soil struck the water. Time after time, the pit retched, its distressed swill bombarded. Cut by flints, the man's hands bled. Obsessed, he toiled on the rim as if he might fill the crater clod by clod, fist by fistful. Then, spent,

114

let his head slump, eyes glazed, his shirt sodden.

Zac crept through the hedge. He was as wet as the farmer. In the gloom, the dog crouched. Tuck looked up. He said nothing. Once before, in the rain, the dog had come through the hedge and watched in that fashion.

'Zac?' Wilfred Tuck shuddered.

It had been their first contact. The mongrel dog had been desperate, alone in the downpour, and followed Tuck homewards. Now, still prone, the dog uttered a peremptory bark and got up. Taking several quick paces, he glanced back, and barked sharply again.

'Leave me, dog.'

Zac persisted.

At last, the man shuffled forward. This time, Zac was the leader, his voice brisk in the vapour, the vague drifting chaos that engulfed farm and farmhouse, and Tuck was following.

Di looked out of her bedroom. There was a tree by the window and she saw little farther, for it was dusk and still raining. She had been crying. For half an hour, head on pillow, she had wept her door bolted.

Blearily now, she fumbled. Tipping the jug on the washstand, she splashed her eyes, then pushed her hair back. It was not just her brother – she had wept, too, for Steve, her fears for him heightened.

Then the call had disturbed her. It had come from outside, like an owl-cry, rain-strangled, and, dropping the face-towel, she went downstairs quickly. Pulling a coat round her shoulders, she sliced into the deluge, the oak looming gauntly, Rose's wash-line tied to it. Di peered in the half-light.

'Over here,' Sal directed.

The bare branches shed water.

'Sal?' Di squinted. The woman was sopping, her thin raiments clinging. 'My God, Sal, find some cover; come under the shedding.'

They stood by the bull pen.

'I brought this for you,' Sal said. She held a cheap metal

trinket, a small cross on a pin. 'Take it, miss, I don't need it. I got used to the grieving.'

'Oh, Sal ...'

'Keep it,' Sal said, 'for I know the pain, lady.'

Di put her arms round her. 'Lord,' she whispered, 'you're wringing! You shouldn't have come – not in this. Where's the toddler?'

'With them – with the Wilsons.'

In the murk, gutters gurgled. 'Of course, I can't take it,' said Di. 'It's yours, Sal, keep it safely. I'll prize the thought ...'

'You've been good to me,' Sal said. It was dark in the buildings, the dank air hay-scented. 'Always treated me decent. And the dog saved the young 'un.' Nearby, the bull snorted. She cringed. 'I can't stop ...'

'Wait.' Di grabbed her. 'He's shut in. There's no danger.'

'Best get back.'

'Tell me something.' She held on to Sal, saying, 'The dog – he did *what*, Sal?'

'On the ice ...' It came slowly. The tinker woman was shy, still in awe of the mongrel. 'I'd not trust him,' she breathed; 'I'd not have him around, for that's no natural creature. He saved the boy, though, I swear it.'

'I didn't know.' Di was silent.

Sal faced into the weather. 'Must get back.' The spume struck her. She turned, still for a second, her thin form contracting, drawn tight in the shadows. 'You've asked where the dog goes. Don't let on that I spoke but Luke could tell a few secrets. Luke's dark. I'd not ask him. There's only trouble in knowing.' Her shape grew dim. 'Luke could tell, though.'

She was gone.

'Sal ...'

Di listened. She could hear the bull's movements and the patter of water. She thought the rain was abating. For a while, the girl lingered, surprised at length to see stars, glad for Sal it had cleared, and for the land, which was swamped.

*

116

The next morning was brilliant. At dawn, Di went to the kale field where her father was working. Tuck was hacking the stems, loading a cart with the plants while Shep set up his hurdles. The growth would go to the cows, the short stumps feed the sheep. Some already were gnawing.

Shep moved the fold forward. 'How's the missus?' he grunted.

'Bearing up.'

He spat pipe juice. Raising a hurdle, he pitched it, driving its shores in the earth. 'Boss was low, took it badly.'

'He'll come through.'

'Has afore - seen some hard days,' Shep told her.

'Takes time.'

'Bloody mess here.' The old man's feet puddled. 'Rained enough for a twelve-month.' He eyed the mud. 'Good lad, Roy was. All the good 'uns are going. Farms littered wi' women.' He looked the girl over. She was, she knew, no oil painting, her eyes baggy, face sleep-starved. Her dungarees needing washing. She could end up in Sal's state. 'Not agin 'em *all*,' Shep said.

'Good to know.'

'In their place, mind.'

'Yes,' she said, 'home with babies!'

She turned her back, passing on, thrusting through the tall kale plants. She was used to Shep's saws. 'Do no harm,' his croak followed, 'if the boss had a grandson.' Damned old fool! Her knees dampened. The air was dry and a wind was blowing, but the leaves retained moisture, silver globules of water which soon soaked her trousers.

'I'll give you a hand, Dad.' She had come with a sickle.

Tuck looked up.

'Until breakfast.'

He nodded. He was, she thought, through the crisis; it would be a slow haul now. She stooped with him, slashing. Tuck paused. 'Better morning . . .'

'Yes,' she said, 'makes a difference.'

'Came up here with him,' Tuck said. 'Last leave - long time back. Didn't talk much, young Roy; never said much,

117

the beggar. Just got on.'

'Knew his mind.'

'He'd have changed things.' Tuck tossed kale to the farmcart. 'He'd have had this place buzzing. Roy was cut out for farming.'

'Yes,' she lied.

'Keen as mustard.'

Di was cold in the tingling breeze. Her legs were wet to the thighs now, the damp creeping up, and she thought of the summer, Roy tall on the haystack. '*When you're here the man's happy*' – her own words remembered.

Roy had frowned. 'When I'm sweating.'

'He's built the farm for you, Roy.'

'Slaved for the farm, Di. I wouldn't.'

She sighed. 'He was brave, Dad.'

'Aye, I've read it, the letter. That was Roy, like they said: made his mind up and did it.' The man moved the horse on. He said with an effort, 'Bloody weeds grow, beasts hunger; nought'll stop, that's for certain. Not the war, not damn all, girl. Let's get this lot carted.'

Shep's dogs ran up, snuffling. They fussed Di. 'Saw Sal Wilson.' She stroked the bitch. 'It's two years since her Tom died. We don't think ...'

Tuck shrugged. 'Reckon.'

'She told me something.' Di brooded. At last, she said, 'Where's the mongrel?'

8

Benson pulled off the road. He was, he told himself grimly, too old to be working. He took a snort from his hip-flask. But for the war, he reflected, he would be in retirement. And how long would the war last? The Bofors gun faced the Vauxhall. The gun had been there an age now, grown into the landscape.

'Mister!' Sal shouted, running.

The doctor eyed her morosely. She was as drab as the gunsite. Once, its sandbags were stout; now their ends drooped and rotted. How many more years of medicine – of rustic births, deaths and backaches – before he fled with his fly-rods to the peace he envisaged?

'It's Luke ...' She looked wretched.

He belched on the liquor. How much more of the killing, how many more local youngsters? Sal's Tom lay in France; there was Roy dead in Norway. He had known them since infants. Who next – Steve? – Benson wondered. He felt a weary compassion.

'Luke?' He wound down the window.

'Luke Wilson,' Sal blurted.

'Well?'

'The man needs a doctor.'

And who did not, thought Doc Benson. That, or more of the whisky, which blunted the war news, blurred the image of carnage. He had served in the first lot. He knew what they looked like: the dead on African sands, the frozen bodies of Russia, the bloated dead of the Atlantic. 'And what's up with Luke Wilson? Can't he get to the surgery?'

'It's his leg,' whined the woman. 'See him now, sir, he's moaning.'

Benson grabbed his bag fiercely. 'Very well, get a move on.' He slid from the car. They *all* moaned, he thought stumbling, lurching over the heather on the bleak uneven ground. So much for the chalk streams, his dream of trout rising! 'Well,' he slurred, 'where's the patient?'

Luke Wilson groaned loudly. The hut was littered with salvage: parts of old cars, wrecked aircraft. Benson blinked, breathing deeply. There was a tail-wheel, its tyre punctured; some kind of a compass; the gearbox off a tractor. The shabby mattress Luke burdened was marked *War Department*. His exposed leg was gory.

'When was *this* done?'

'Few days back.'

'And you've left it in this state?' Doc Benson leaned closer; the sight of blood was bracing. The tooth wounds were savage. Someone's dog had been thorough. 'You're a bloody fool, Wilson.'

'Sweet Jesus, don't touch it!'

'Looks angry. Where were you?' Benson stroked his moustache, moved by Luke's, 'In the forest,' to curl his lip drily. The sneer was sardonic. Sal had crept to a corner. Scared, she cringed from the doctor. 'Got hot water?' he queried. 'Fetch it, woman, I'll need some.' He wrenched his bag open. 'Forest, eh?' he derided.

'It's true,' the man whimpered.

'More likely, caught thieving.'

'Swear to Christ, in the forest.' Benson saw his eyes widen. 'In the deep where the swamps are. There's no law agin that, sir, least no law of this kingdom, for the landlord's the devil. Aye, and ghouls for his keepers. Dear Mother, you're hurting!'

He jerked the leg, turning pale.

Benson said, 'Hold it still. You should mend your ways, Wilson.'

'I done nothing, for Christ's sake.'

'You're a mess.'

'He came at me. In the depths, sir, the wet place.'

'Keep still!'

'On my soul ...'

'Damn your soul,' drawled Doc Benson. Sal had fetched

120

him a basin. 'I'm not concerned with your soul. You're a trespassing villain; not surprising you're bitten. I'll clean this and bind it.' When he was done, he said brusquely, 'That's a temporary dressing.'

'Thanks, mister,' Sal told him.

'Never mind that,' he blustered. 'See he gets in for treatment.' He looked back from the doorway. 'Man,' said Benson, his head shaking, 'you must *really* have upset him. I've seen a few dog-bites – that fellow meant business.' He returned to the Vauxhall and lit a cigarette. For a time, he sat musing, tobacco ash spilling, then drove to the farm lane.

Tuck was on the new tractor. The field he was ploughing, unturned in a lifetime, was a stern test of metal. Thick with tough-rooted vetch, anchored deep in the subsoil, it resented disturbance. Shep had thought the scheme dotty. 'Yon's not ploughland; ye'll rue it.' But more food was needed. There was two pounds in grants for each acre of grass turned. Tuck ploughed, while the gulls wheeled.

Benson stopped at the hedgeside. Getting out, he stood watching. Flights of starlings shoaled over like fish in grey water. The farmer rode twisting sideways, his rearward glance worried. The field grasses were matted, their ancient roots stubborn, concealing obstructions unknown to the ploughman.

At times, the furrow wheel slithered. Now, the roots won the battle and Tuck swung down cursing, hands tearing and tugging. Then the big man remounted and, dropping the share-points, drove on, plough-breasts glinting, the small engine snorting.

Benson stepped through the field gate. Something made him look down, perhaps the bright eyes which pierced him, inquiring his purpose. Zac was curled in the gicks, quietly guarding Tuck's Thermos, which lay with the tool-box.

'How's the boss?' Benson paused. He returned the dog's interest and Zac stretched, his tail stirring. They crossed the meadow together to stand at the furrows. Some were rough, with grass still showing. They would need further working but the start was successful, the air rich with loam smells.

Gulls swooped, red mouths gaping. As they gorged on the lugworms, the tractor came forward. Tuck's begrimed cap was slanted, his eyes concentrating. Abruptly, the plough screamed, and for a moment, sparks fountained. Then Tuck dismounted and was wrestling the flintstone. He saw Benson. 'No damage!'

'New tool, Wilf?'

'Time we had one.' Tuck regarded the ridges. The gritty topsoil was black, root infested, but the loam stood up plumply, a lubricous umber that swelled to the headland. It was not fine horse-ploughing – nor half of the labour. The girl could have done it. He touched the hydraulic lever. 'That's the trick, power-lift,' Tuck said. It beat the Case, with her drag-plough. 'It's the future,' he grunted, 'it's what Roy would have reckoned.'

Benson proffered his hip-flask.

'Keeping well in yourself, Wilf?'

'Don't need *that*,' said the farmer.

'Good sign. My God, I do.'

'Bloody quack,' Tuck said mildly. Zac watched as he climbed back on the tractor. The dog displayed a quiet patience, a resolve, thought Doc Benson, to wait if need be till doomsday. Benson stowed the flask slowly. Could the mongrel be vicious?

'Seen the Wilsons round lately?'

'Not since Di set them hedging!' Tuck throttled the tractor. It lurched. 'Why?' he shouted.

'Thought they might have been snooping.' Benson shrugged. 'Know what Luke is ...'

'Luke Wilson!'

She glimpsed the man from the forge but had to wait for the towbar. The smith was still cackling. 'Young Jim's two-foot taller.' The thought tickled Rutter. 'Ye'd think he'd beaten yon Rommel ...'

Di peered after the tinker.

' ... not just sat on a tractor!'

'Aye.' She turned, her voice impatient. 'Poor Jim,' she said

122

quickly, 'like a dog with two tails now.'

'You'd best watch him,' growled Rutter. He grinned, his lips smutty. 'He could cause some destruction. You'd best watch that tractor.'

'We'll take care. Is the bar done?'

The smith raked the forge coals. 'Tuppence short on a shilling, young Jim, but well-meaning. The towbar? Aye, the beggar's here somewhere.' He rummaged in corners. 'I done her, don't worry.'

'Oh, come on,' Di said tersely.

'You'll be in a hurry?'

'To catch Luke,' she told him.

'Then you'll *need* to look slippy. Here' – he swooped – 'knew I done her.' He took the bar to the truck and, when Di was in, grunted, 'Catch Luke? Some would like to!'

She started the Morris. The wintry road was deserted and the girl eyed the village. It stared back from dark windows, taciturn and suspicious. A fire burned at the schoolhouse. She watched the smoke from the chimney. It writhed then dissolved, like Luke Wilson.

Beside her, Zac nosed the windscreen.

'Down!' she snapped, driving slowly. 'If he spots *you* we've lost him.' She braked. 'Down, Zac, damn you!'

Luke was back in view, limping. She got out close behind him. The street was bleak, raw and silent, so quiet Rutter's hammer, now distant, resounded. 'Luke, I wanted to see you ...'

He turned, his eyes staring.

Di said, 'Sal mentioned something – you know where the dog goes.'

'Dog?' He backed away, fumbling.

'I'd like to know.' A cart passed them. The pub was near, and Luke eyed it.

'Between *us*, Luke, no further.'

'Where's the cur?' Luke was shaking.

She watched him dive for the ale-room and stop; the door was bolted. For a moment, he leaned there, a thin human buttress, and Di said, frustrated, 'Come on, I won't eat you.

123

Bloody hell, we can talk, man.'

'Talk?' His glance was suspicious.

'Sure, Luke, what's so secret?'

'I know nothing, no secrets.'

She smiled, her gleam piercing. 'Let's just chat.' Luke
eased slightly. They were alone and Tuck's daughter, moving
casually closer, placed her back to the pub wall, hands in
pockets, still smiling. 'Sal's all right, Luke, I like her.' She
eyed him. 'She's helpful.'

He scowled.

'*Truthful*,' Di said.

'What's she told you?'

Di stiffened. The truck's horn was skirling. Zac had
climbed on the seat and, chest nudging the button, raised a
wail from the klaxon. 'Luke!' But Luke did not tarry. Like a
rabbit, he bolted, unrestrained by the limp, and Di shouted,
'Oh, run then – I'll find out next time, Wilson!'

She dragged back to the Morris. As the man's footfalls
faded, a plane droned in the heavens. It was high, faint but
nagging. For a while, it persisted, drawn it seemed to the
village, then, with blowfly whim, vanished.

They passed in dozens that evening.

'Do you think they're ours?' Rose said. It was hard to be
certain, for the RAF had grown stronger, its own night raids
mounting.

Tuck cleaned the shotgun in silence. Di was combing the
mongrel. She almost hoped they were German, for the
thought of Steve up there was frightening. Unanswered,
Rose checked the curtains. 'We'll know tomorrow,' she
murmured.

Know the worst, Di reflected. And the worst from the
desert, where Rommel was charging, his tanks in Benghazi.
She said, shunting her war-cares, 'It's the hare-shoot on
Friday.'

'Huh,' said Tuck.

'You'll not go, then?'

'Never does,' Rose said.

'Plenty will,' the man told them. Tuck had never shot hares. He was fond of the creatures and often watched them while working. Shot, they screamed like young children. He did not grudge them some turnips – nor the birds what he owed *them* in God's sight, he reckoned, for human greed riled him.

Rabbits, Tuck chased with venom. He was hard, too, on pigeons, in part for their numbers. Both species abounded, one a blight on his pasture, the other on green-stuff fed in winter to cattle. That, perhaps, was the difference. Tuck would not see his cows robbed.

He looked up as the telephone rang and Di whirled out through the doorway.

'Steve!' Her voice reached the parlour.

Tuck eyed Rose in the lamplight. Neither spoke; his wife was shadowed, her face to the fire, but he knew what she thought. Why not *Roy*? Her head lifted. 'Steve,' she said, 'that's a blessing. The poor girl's been anxious.'

He got up with the shotgun.

For a moment, Zac brightened, then, the gun shelved, lost interest.

'She'll be pleased.' Rose was listening. 'Good to hear her laugh, Wilfred.'

The planes had gone when the chat stopped, the girl flushed from talking. 'He's been posted, new squadron. No more ops for the present,' she summarized quietly. 'Sent his best, Dad. And you, Ma. Says it's boring, more training, but at least he'll be safer. Towing gliders – *sounds* safer.'

'Aye,' said Tuck.

'Do they feed him?'

Di smiled. 'Never asked, Ma.'

'Lord above!' Rose reproved her. Tuck's wife eyed Roy's picture. 'Men like Steve need full bellies.'

'Well, I'll tell him you said so.' Di touched Rose on the shoulder. 'Next time,' she said fondly.

Tuck went out to the horses. He flashed his lamp on their halters. All well, he stood smoking, watching clouds cross the moon. They were racing, conveying, in the moon's ring, a wild flight through the darkness; night spirits. His pipe glowed.

Indoors, Rose was moving, making the fire safe. When he came back in, she told him, 'Di's gone up. She'll sleep happy.'

'She's stuck on Steve.'

'Is that bad?'

'God knows, Rosie.'

'Could be a clerk or a salesman.' She drew near, her tone becoming reflective. 'She'd be off if it was, Tuck; they'd not stay to grow 'taters. Steve we know.' Her voice murmured. 'He'd be more like a son. They'd stay on, run the farm ...'

'Aye, maybe.' Tuck embraced her.

Zac was curled on the hearth rug. He yawned, close to slumber. It was late, pushing ten. 'Maybe,' Tuck said. Only daybreak was certain – another day, renewed labours. And more dead on the war fronts.

Part Three

THE FOREST

1

The Summer Fair drew a crowd. It was a drab one, war-jaded, but had come to be counted. Old men filled the tap-rooms. Tilted over their tankards, they glowered, their stubble beer-frothed. Commoners of the forest, they had ancient concessions – rights to graze their beasts freely – and long recollections.

Once, the fair had been lively; the sound of animals, rousing. Now, with the younger men missing, the festival languished. Prodding pigs, trotting horses, the country people appeared weary. Youth's passion was absent and even the livestock, few in number, were torpid.

Sal sat on the pub bench, holding a glass in both hands. The fair was her annual outing, an occasion for tinkers, whose families met there. Luke was trotting a pony. Forest men stood around, unimpressed by the creature. Cow-hocked, it fetched little – and that quickly squandered as Luke got drunk on the proceeds.

Each year, selling ponies, the tinker clans tippled until, by the fair's end they were ready for trouble. Then, with weasel malevolence, they would take to the woodside – befuddled Wilsons and Fowlers, old family feudsmen – to pursue their vendettas.

When the inn closed, Sal dithered. She had hoped Luke would be handy to see her home, out of danger. Instead, a thin youth approached, grown lascivious with boozing, and began to molest her. At first, she tried to elude him. She knew his people were Fowlers, and what could develop.

Breath beery, he grabbed her. The screech Sal raised was spontaneous, a cat's squall of anguish. What came next ran to pattern.

Pounced on by the Wilsons, the youth outvied Sal in screaming until, punched, his lips thickened. The Fowlers rallied. Sal fled. Around her, clansmen were grouping, obscene in their insults, the women fiery with liquor. Dusk was falling. She could see Luke, his arms flailing, and the pride of the Fowlers, a peg-legged, pot-bellied veteran, fighting drunk.

She ran wildly, her hair tangling. Shapes loomed, clawing vixens, beer-crazed Fowler females whom she dodged, her feet flying. Sal sped on through the twilight. At the wood's edge, she paused. Now, the cries were less strident, the partisans distant. Black-etched on the woodland, demon dancers, they skirmished.

For a trice, a blade glinted. Peg-leg Fowler was roaring. She could hear the man's curses. He had his back to the tree-bole, leg removed, the peg brandished, swung high as a cudgel. Around him, foes cowed and forayed. Sal lurched on by the forest.

She scarcely knew which was worse, her panting dread of the drunkards or her fear of the trees. She was stumbling now. Unseen, Zac stole beside her, parallel through the shadows, eyes sharp, a grey escort.

Tuck went to the bull pen. It was hot; the dung steamed and the sun drew bright furrows through gaps in the buildings. Thatched roofs teemed with sparrows. Man and beast faced each other. Both were large, each was stubborn. 'No pranks; watch your manners.'

The bull's wet nose snuffled.

Tuck looped the rope round thick horns and took it down through the ring, his voice benign, gruffly soothing. Hitching the end to a rail, he fetched the short chain-linked nose lead and called for assistance. 'Jim!' Nobody answered. 'Where's the fathead?' he muttered.

Rose was hanging out washing. It was hard, in the summer, to keep enough clothes clean. Now the rush-time had started – hay, the harvest, muck-carting – finding soap was a nightmare. The ration was paltry, barely keeping their hands washed.

'Jim!' She heard Tuck call twice.

'He's gone down to the poultry.'

'Damn the oaf!'

Rose pegged sheets. 'Don't blame Jim,' she called shrilly, 'I sent him. They needed mash and more grit. He took the oyster shell with him.'

'Damn the beggar, I need him.'

'What for?' She was sweating. She had emptied the basket and walked round towards him. Tuck had come from the buildings. He said, 'I'm turning the bull out. It'll take two to lead him. It's a step to the field and he'll likely be uppish.'

Rose stopped. 'You're daft, Wilfred!'

'He'll behave in the meadow.'

'Hurt someone, for God's sake.'

'They'd have no right to be there; there's no footpath,' he answered. 'Besides,' he growled, 'he's worse penned. He'll be content with the heifers. It's getting him down there ...'

'You'll not let that lad help you!' The woman glared fiercely. It was a festering subject. 'If you're mad, that's your business; you'll not risk the boy, Tuck.'

'Risk, be damned!'

'I'll not argue.' She turned, her skirt swirling. 'You don't learn,' she fired backwards, her steps brisk in departure. 'You're mad, Tuck, a madman!'

'Bloody fowls!' Tuck stood cursing.

He retraced his steps slowly, surprised by a motor. The Jeep stopped abruptly. Still fuming, he waited. The young man who dismounted was alone and in uniform. 'Guess I'm lost,' said the stranger, 'not used to your lanes yet.' He gazed round. 'Still a greenhorn. Only landed a week back.'

'A Yank?' Tuck's eyes narrowed.

'US Army – advance guard.'

'Took your time!'

'Guess you're busy ...'

'Damn right.' Tuck surveyed him. Two years late and lost already! The boy wore light steel-framed glasses and his uniform was tailored. So spruce was his turnout, so pristine, Tuck reckoned, he might have come for a tea-dance, not a war. Not a dung-yard! And yet, thought Tuck, he was sturdy. 'Got a beast to be shifting.' He paused, his glance artful. 'Tag on, I'll direct you.'

'Be pleased.'

'Used to cattle?'

The soldier smiled. 'I'm no cowboy.'

'Would you just hold the rope, son? I'm going to clip on the lead then we'll stroll nice and easy. The old bull's no trouble. Just keep abreast, take the slack up.'

'Jeez!'

The bull lurched, head shaking.

'You all right?' Tuck glanced sideways.

The other whistled, his brows raised. 'That's one heck of a steak, sir!'

'Aye.' The great beast rolled forward. 'Steady, lad, hold him steady.' Tuck strained. 'Easy does it.' He liked the nerve of the Yank, innocent though he might be. The shorthorn was daunting. 'We'll make a cattleman of you! What part do you come from?'

'New York State.'

'Where you bound for?'

'Southampton,' the boy said.

'We'll put you right.' The bull bellowed. 'Whoa, beast, ye'll soon be there. Few more steps, damn your caper.' Tuck swayed, then caught his balance. He braced. 'Loose the gate latch. Take the rope from him, mister. Stand back now, I've got him.' The bull paused, feet on turf, and the man slipped the chain lead. 'That'll suit him,' Tuck grunted.

They leaned on the toprail. 'They're not going to believe this.' The young American grinned. 'The guys will *not* believe this one!' He bent to Zac, who had followed. 'I'll take the dog, sir,' he jested.

'It would cost you Fort Knox, son.'

'He's a pal?'

'You're damned right.'

Di approached. 'You've a nerve, Dad!' She considered the stranger. 'The bull could've killed him!'

'Bah!' said Tuck, 'the boy's useful.'

'He doesn't *know* the brute, does he?'

Tuck beamed. 'He enjoyed it. The lad comes from good stock – Pilgrim Fathers,' he blustered.

Di glowered. 'The old bastard.' Tuck had left for the sheep fold. She eyed the GI with interest. 'Was he right?'

'No,' he told her, 'my forebears were German. Is the bull really dangerous?'

'It had Dad down. Zac saved him.' His surprise made her chuckle. He shared the joke, quietly laughing, his amusement self-mocking, unlike her screen-fostered notions of American brashness.

'So I could've been wounded, shipped home as a hero!'

'Don't say that.' She smiled gravely, for it could happen yet, Di thought: that, or worse. He was Roy's age. 'Don't wish yourself injury. What job did you come from?'

'I was studying.'

'College?'

'Post-graduate history.'

'There's a bit around these parts.' She was reminded of London, the kind of fellows she had met there. 'The forest is ancient. You'll take the road which runs past it.'

He said, 'The ancient New Forest!' and laughed. 'Guess that's Britain! Didn't Saxon kings hunt there? It must be more than eight centuries since it came under *new* law – last time you were conquered.'

'Aye,' said Di, 'by the Normans. And the woods got their own back.' She called Zac. 'They're revengeful.'

'You mean, Richard and Rufus?'

'Both died in the forest; both sons of the Conqueror.' It was her best hand of history. She said, before he could trump it, 'One gored by a stag, the other pierced by an arrow. It's not a place that likes strangers.'

'I'll pass, I'm an ally.' The boy's smile was open. He was, she thought, like Steve, candid. Not that Steve would have said, as the Yank did, grin widening, 'It's for sure, trees aren't stupid; Aristotle knew that much. He said trees have perception. He also said they had passion.'

They had stopped where the Jeep stood. The dog quizzed the soldier.

'No kidding,' he added, 'I truly like forests. I'm going to lap up this journey.'

'Just stick to the highway.'

'No stags and no arrows!'

'No explorations.' She was earnest. 'Get bogged down and you've had it. There's no help in the forest and the ground is deceptive.' As he left, she watched, calling, 'Just remember, be careful!'

They met again after harvest. Di and Zac were in Ringwood when he came through the market. Alamein had been fought, the Americans had landed, and all the talk on the wireless was of African victory. It seemed a long way from Hampshire. 'Hi,' he said, pleased to see her. 'I've been hoping to find you. I forgot something last time.'

'Oh!' They stood by the pens.

'To ask your name,' he said brightly.

His was Greg.

Zac surveyed him. Men passed wearing gaiters, and some inquired after Tuck who, Di told them, was busy. 'Carting muck,' she reported, 'I'm running his errands.' They eyed the soldier and Di twinkled.

She had come by the forest, its autumnal shades fiery. 'You found the road then?' she asked him.

'Sure, those old oaks were friendly.'

'I remember – tree worship!'

He laughed, slapping a pig. The creature grunted and slobbered. Greg pondered the farm crowd. 'Well, maybe,' he reflected. 'Beneath our skins, we're all pagans.'

'Don't worry,' the girl said. 'Things don't change much in these parts.'

He eyed her frankly. 'Nor should they. The fall here's a glory. They had it figured, the ancients, seeking God in the trees. Today, we worship our bankrolls and pulp trees for money.'

'Yes, well . . .'

His eyes lingered.

'Some,' said Di, 'need the money. I'm going to the auction, we've a beast in the sale ring.'

'Not the *bull*?'

It amused her. Striding out, she guffawed, the man and dog walking with her. 'Dad won't sell *that* old bugger, not till somebody's battered.' She shook her head. 'That'll happen. One day, there'll be trouble.'

At the ring, dealers squinted. Lowing beasts glared, their eyes rolling. Pawing straw, they looked dismal, sick of the business, Greg reckoned. He sat with Di among herdsmen; ignored on the benches, Zac sprawled where their legs touched. Attention homed on the cattle. 'Bloody misers,' Di muttered.

'Not the price you expected?'

'The misers!'

He smiled. 'The pub's open. What the hell, Di, we've landed! Have a beer on the Yanks!' He bought pints and two pies. Looking thoughtful, he asked her, 'Guess there's someone you go with – a guy in the forces?'

She nodded. 'Air-gunner.'

He said. 'Yeah,' and they brooded.

'There's a long way ahead, Greg, all Europe to fight for. Africa's just a start. Any damn thing could happen.'

'It's luck. He'll be lucky.'

'And you?'

'I'm no flier.' He shrugged, cramped for arm-room. Farmers crowded the bar, joined by grey-visaged merchants, ageing seedsmen and stockmen. The girl grabbed a table. 'Eat the pie, Greg, it's warm.'

Like the beer, thought the soldier. He regarded her

quietly. Her tan alone helped the stuff down. She was easy to look at and simple to talk to, a girl of no-nonsense. He watched her feed Zac a crust, the slim hand strong from farm work.

'Your dad's fond of the dog.'

'To put it mildly.' She brightened. It was an easier subject. 'Zac's a brick.' The dog blinked. 'You'd not guess how we got him.' They relaxed and the dog settled. Once or twice, his eyes flickered, dark, watchful. Then he slumbered.

2

The earth shuddered. Zac had stopped on the track. Tuck had yet to take notice but the mongrel, ears keener, was already attentive. He saw the horse top the brow and plunge on, the cart rocking.

The mare was one of Zac's favourites. Only broken that spring, she had grown up with him near her, often dossed in her bed-straw. Zac had see her first bridled, first led out with a bit in, eyes blinkered. The dog had helped reassure her.

Now, she raced like a charger, the farm cart a chariot. 'By God' – Tuck had stiffened – 'I'll choke the youth, wring his neck off!'

Down the field the mare thundered, reins flying, hooves drumming. Jim had taken the cart out but was no longer with it. The horse advanced like a bronco, as if never harnessed.

She had plunged like that when Tuck broke her. Then, the young mare had fought him, rearing up, leaping forward while the man, scrambling and crouching, had clutched the lines, the rope searing. At last, the pair of them sweating, horse and man had drawn closer, reaffirming their friendship, the dog there, tail wagging.

And so Tuck had continued, skill matched against horse-power. There had been many tussles. Hitched first to a log, to introduce her to pulling, the young horse had panicked, entangling the traces. Zac had watched the man free her. Somehow, her hooves missed him.

Next, with shafts at her shoulders, the mare had learned cart work. 'Gently, mare,' Tuck had rasped. 'We'll try you out on soft-going.' The maiden haul had proved hectic: a lunging, rip-snorting sprint, after which she stood fuming, incensed and unbudging. In the end, she had mellowed, a strong, willing toiler.

Until now, when she was galloped. 'God,' moaned Tuck, 'she'll be crippled!' Hooves thumped and the cart bounced, its loose tailboard crashing.

Now, the mare neared the track, heading straight for the field gate. There was a jerk, and a post splintered. One wheel-knave had rammed it. Stunned, the horse reeled and halted, was flung on her haunches then got up, her flanks trembling.

'Hold still, damn it; my God, don't run on, lass!' Tuck prayed.

The animal's eyes rolled. Twice, she tossed her head, frightened, about to take off anew when the mongrel dog reached her. Calmly, Zac stood before her, nose raised, a paw lifted. The hill of lathered flesh dwarfed him. Then, her great nostrils flaring, the mare slowly stretched downwards, breathing Zac's cool assurance.

'Gently, lass.' Tuck came forward. He stroked the sopping neck, crooning, 'You're all right, the old dog's here. Whoa, my girl, take it gently.'

'She took fright,' Jim said, looming.

'Right you are,' Tuck said grimly, 'and so will you, my lad, next time. You're lucky she's standing, nothing harmed but a gatepost. Come here; hold the mare still.'

He ran a hand down her legs. There was no sign of damage.

'It weren't my fault.' The boy pouted. 'She took off wi'out warning.'

'Without warning be hell-damned! There's only one rule with horses – it says it's *always* your fault, lad.'

'Well,' sulked Jim, 'she's a handful. The mare's off at nothing.'

'She's young. Christ Almighty, you'll find out what's a handful when you start taking girls out! She's young, lad; aye, and female!' Tuck sighed. He said, 'Watch her. Take her back, boy, and watch her.'

He frowned, staring upwards. The farm lad was craning. High above them, an aircraft, a British bomber, flew westward. It trailed a long, sagging towline, as if dragging a breakdown. Tuck gawped. It was novel. At the end of the line flew a second large aircraft, a ship without engines.

136

Jim's face glowed. 'Boss, a glider!'

Tuck scowled. 'Bloody warplanes.'

'Full of soldiers,' Jim told him. The boy had heard others talking. 'She'll land in a garden. Tow her out to a battle, she'll glide down packed with soldiers.'

'Hold that mare!'

'Heck, a glider!'

'How's she flying, tail-gunner?'

'In high-tow, sailing smoothly.' Like a plywood box, Steve thought. They had climbed from the airfield. As they levelled for cruising, the glider nosed downwards. Bucking through the tug's slipstream, it regained stable motion in the low-tow position.

Steve could watch it below him. The big Horsa was ugly, a black bug in the blue with a greenhouse-like cockpit. He could see its two pilots, army sergeants. They waved. Steve waggled the Brownings.

He could hear their chat crackling. 'Last hop – roll on Friday.' Then the course would be over. The Halifax lumbered. Its skipper's voice cut in crisply. 'I'll drink to that, Matchbox!'

Steve unscrewed his tea Thermos. The towline drooped as the glider yawed. Far beneath them, scarred ramparts, the South Downs of England met the sprawl of dark forest. He drank the tea, his mind roving.

Dearest Di, leave on Friday ...

He had forgotten to post it; he would phone her that evening. Five more days back at Murton with the girl and the mongrel! That was Steve's dream of England – a land that stuck to your fingers, balled your boots, smelled of tractors – not the map spread below him.

'Tug to Matchbox ...'

'Got you – over.'

'Coming up to the zone now.'

He kept his eyes on the glider. Its pilots were peering. He heard one through the static: 'Understood. We're releasing. Thanks for the lift, tug, we'll see you.' The towline fell from the Horsa. Steve grinned, sticking a thumb up and saw them acknowledge. Then the glider had banked, and was sliding down, dwindling.

'All clear, skip,' he reported.

'Home, James!' They turned slowly, in a wide arc, engines pounding. Another Halifax passed them. Other tugs were returning and below, on the downland, Steve could see several gliders, like toys, safely landed. Around them, soldiers were moving. Steve relaxed. They looked antlike, just starting their manoeuvres.

Poor sods! he thought, and munched a sandwich with relish. The rear turret vibrated. He was used to its quirks and the cramping discomfort. It was better than marching. Crew-chat blipped in his headphones. He could hear Stenton whistling. The tune was *Waltzing Matilda*. The new man was an Aussie – that, and tone-deaf, Steve reckoned.

They flew on above cloudbanks. It was quiet for a moment then a voice said, 'Damned oil, skip. One and two. Pressure's dropping.'

Steve moaned. Bloody engines! They had lost good lads lately through fires in the motors, one crate burning on take-off, the whole thing exploding. He listened. Terse words crackled.

'How's she read?'

'Piss-poor, skipper.'

It seemed remote, a world from him, but he could feel the changed pulse and knew the screws had been feathered, that the plane was on half-power now. His last hop before furlough!

Dear Di, cross your fingers! Have a word with Zac for me! He had planned to help Tuck, see the old Case was healthy. *She* had never betrayed him; never lost power while working. Thank God, base was handy.

'Number three's looking dicey.'

Perhaps those soldiers knew something, their feet on good loamy farmland. The other gunner still whistled. He struck Steve as a nut and, when the man wormed back grinning, the

138

opinion was hardened. 'Got a wad?' Stenton bawled it. 'Forgot to bring any tucker!'

Steve gave him a sandwich.

'Thanks, mate. Feeling peckish.' Stenton groped in a pocket and drew a small white mouse from it. The Aussie beamed. 'So's Matilda.' Far below, the earth tilted. A distant runway slewed with it. Stenton's mouse nibbled bread-crumbs. 'Thanks, sport, that was needed. Christ, those engines sound knackered!'

He went off with his mouth full and, when at last they had landed – a fire tender beside them, the blood-wagon racing – Stenton roared, still unruffled, 'Lucky mascot, Matilda, I'd not fly without her!'

Steve climbed down. He was sticky. He dumped his 'chute without speaking and walked on, reflecting. The canteen was crowded and others mentioned the landing. 'Bloody drama production!'

He sniffed. 'Change a shilling?'

Someone forked out the coppers. 'Go on, send her our love, Steve!'

He shoved the coins in the phone-box. 'Di . . .' He paused, her voice eager. 'No,' he said, 'no excitement. Training hops, old folks' outings. Listen, Di, see you Friday – five days' leave – can you meet me? Afternoon, at the station. Tell the boss I'm arriving. And tell Zac he's been rumbled.'

'What?'

'I've rumbled his secret.'

'He's here.'

'Just you tell him! See you then, at the station . . .'

Di came with the Morris. It had rained throughout the journey and teemed down as he met her. The railway office gave them shelter. There had, he thought, been a rainstorm the first time he had seen her, on Di's arrival from London. She had stunned him – still stunned him.

'Wait, Steve, the truck's leaking.'

'It always leaked.' He surveyed her. Her hair dripped, she

139

was field-soiled. But Tuck's daughter was vibrant. There was a charge in the girl that was like a magneto: she sent a tingling shock through him.

She looked outside. 'It's too heavy.'

They paused while it thundered. The station hall was a hen coop. Steve scarcely noticed the grate, filled with stained cigarette-ends, or the dowdy war posters. *Careless Talk Costs Lives,* one said. *Walls have ears.* They were flaking. Lightning flashed and the window, little more than a peephole, turned eerily brilliant.

Five days! He breathed deeply.

'Tuck's waiting,' she told him, as the rain drubbed. 'Steve, he's frantic. The axle's gone on the Fergy.'

'What you need's a mechanic!'

'I've fetched a spare, can you fix it?' The airman grinned and she added, 'God, I sound like him, don't I? Poor Steve, what a welcome!' She held his arm. A bell jangled. In the gloom, no one answered and Di said, 'But you're *needed.* You can see how we miss you!'

'I've missed you.' He embraced her.

They drew apart as the door swung and a man hauled in from the deluge. He was stooped, his clothes streaming, and he glowered wretchedly at them. Snatching a box, he departed. Di giggled. Alone again, they stood laughing.

'Where's Zac?'

'With Dad,' Di said.

'Well, I've cracked it. No kidding.'

'No?' She looked disbelieving.

'I've rumbled him,' Steve said.

'A little bird told you?'

'A little mouse,' he said, teasing.

Thunder rolled and she frowned. 'I've tried Luke – Luke's not telling.' There was a flash and she flinched. The bang brought tar down the chimney. For a moment the sky raged then, brightening, grew docile. 'Well?' she said.

Steve was earnest. 'I'd take a bet – I think the dog came by air, Di.'

*

Zac headed for Murton. Moist, the sky gleamed and springs in spate washed the roadsides. Many tracks of the region, based on ancient brook courses, quickly flooded in cloudbursts. Zac splashed, stepping quickly.

He still limped on a foreleg. The slight defect in the limb gave a roll to his action. Age had added some stiffness, the first hint of hip problems, but the mongrel was lively. Like a bird's, his coat glistened; like a magpie's, bold-patterned.

At the sheepfold, he halted. Shep's big drover swore quietly. The mongrel glared but truce bound them and the bitch, her eyes brazen, came to flirt; soon upbraided.

'Let him be,' bawled the shepherd, 'come'ee here, dang the beggar!'

Zac looked back. Trees were dripping. Marching on to the village, he turned in at Doc Benson's. Beyond the surgery entrance, the kitchen door beckoned. He scraped a paw down its frame and sat waiting. It opened.

'Here – and take it away, dog!' Benson's housekeeper fretted. She tossed a bone to the mongrel. 'Don't you let Doctor catch you; he'd fair roast me, old Benson!'

The dog lay by the garage. The bone was small, from mean rations, and Zac quickly crunched it. Next, he stopped at the school-house. He could hear children singing. He listened, tail stirring. Zac was fond of the kids but they had lessons to sit through. As he mooched on, rustics hailed him. He was well-known in the village.

At the shop, he cadged biscuits.

The smith was shovelling his forge clean.

'On the loose?' Rutter grunted. He hurled out dung and grey clinker. 'You watch your step,' said the blacksmith.

The man rolled tobacco. Luke had shown him the toothmarks. The Wilsons were vengeful. He took his tongs to the fire and lit up from an ember. 'Just mind your step and stay farmside.' Luke's threats had been vicious. The smith eyed the mongrel.

For a while, the dog pondered. Then he stretched. He was restive, glancing first back through Murton then ahead to the hutment.

141

Rutter puffed. 'Hey . . .' he muttered.

Zac was off.

'*Home*, you beggar!' The blacksmith shrugged, his words unheeded. The brute was worse than his master – neither Tuck nor Zac listened!

3

Tuck sharpened the hay-knife. The open rick by the dairy was old, sweet and mellow. Compressed, the hay cut like tobacco. Bestride the pungent brown layers, he pumped the curved blade two-handed, thrusting down between his boots, edging gradually sideways.

'She's not right,' wheezed the cowman. 'The machine isn't right yet.' He glanced up, buckets rattling. Zac had strayed. Tuck was tetchy – alway was with the dog gone. 'Not right,' the man echoed.

The farmer ignored him. Shoulders wide, a colossus, he plunged the knife and the hay ripped. Knack and muscle were needed. Tuck had faith in strong sinew. Machinery beat him. They had at last filled the craters. The bulldozer had roared – all fifteen tons of the monster – and left more mess than the bombs had.

'Damn the blamed machine, cowman!' He put his stone to the knife. 'Don't I pay you for milking?'

The other sneered. '*Pay*, you call it?' Calves were sucking at milk pails. One was Brindle's grand-daughter. 'Not for curing contraptions!'

The tawny calf looked up, dribbling. She had her grand-dam's sharp features, the keen eye, the quick interest. 'B'God,' wailed Tuck, 'you're the fellow, it's your business, the dairy.'

Shoving the stone in his belt, he drove the sharpened blade so fiercely it could have severed an ankle. The old hay smelled like treacle. It was dark as Shep's pipe shag, and Tuck cut it squarely, forking off as he went so the shelf became lower.

'See Steve's back,' said the cowman. He scratched his head, one eye closing. 'Steve's a way with machines, boss; he could likely correct it.'

'Steve's mending the Fergy.' Tuck stabbed down, his lips

143

tightening. 'The lad's busy,' he grunted.

'When he's done ...'

The blade burrowed.

Steve arrived on the tractor. He pulled up, smile complacent. 'There she is – new half-axle. She'll do a while longer.' He jumped off, looking grubby. Making steps for the Case, he exclaimed, 'That's *my* lady: you've never caught *her* in trouble!'

'They're *all* trouble,' Tuck told him; 'all machines are damned trouble.' He slid down from the haystack. 'Bearings seized, busted axles. Can't do right with the beggars.'

'I'd say she'd seen a few seasons.'

'Reconditioned, they reckoned.' Tuck forked the hay briskly.

'Still a good tool, don't worry.'

The cowman said, 'We've more trouble.' He squinted, voice wheedling. 'With the dairy machine, son.'

'Damn it,' Tuck fumed, 'get on, man!' He jabbed the prongs in the fodder. 'Blamed old fool,' he said darkly, 'never done with his moaning.' He humped the hay to the buildings, looking round. 'It would help, lad ... don't suppose you'd have time, though ...'

Steve grinned. 'Aye, I'll check it. Stop the old fellow grousing!'

'Be obliged.' Tuck was thankful. He dumped the load, saying gruffly, 'B'God, you'd be more use here, boy, than up with those gliders. I'm too old for new playthings.'

He broke off and Steve told him, 'Good tool, boss, the Fergy. Hydraulics – the future.'

Tuck paused. He said, 'Future? I lost the future with Roy, son.'

'There's Di.'

'While the war lasts.' Tuck looked glum. 'The girl's helping. She'll be gone when it's over.'

'No,' said Steve, 'she'll be married.'

Tuck leaned on the pitchfork. 'I've to hear the girl say so.' He regarded the weaners. They stretched up, legs splayed, snuffling. He could have listed their forebears name by name since he started. The herd was a life's work.

He peered sideways, eyes hooded. 'She's afraid, son – can't blame her – of the war, being widowed.'

'It's a risk. More's the hurry.'

'I'd not stop you.'

'I've asked her.'

'Asked?' the farmer said slowly. 'You'll get nowhere by asking, not with Di. She needs telling. Fix a date, lad, and *tell* her.' It had worked with her mother. He shook his head, saying grimly, 'Next thing, damn it, we'll lose her; some pen-pusher will thieve her. Or a Yank,' the man brooded.

In the house later, Rose said, 'About the dog, Steve. Di tells me ...'

They sat back with their teacups and Tuck said, 'He's missing. You know he's off again?'

'Yes, Wilf. Just let's listen to Steve now.' Rose turned to the airman. 'Do you really believe it? Do they take dogs up flying?'

'Of course not!' Tuck told her.

Di put in, 'But remember, Zac came near the start, Dad. Things were more free and easy. Phoney War. Am I right, Steve?'

'More a lark.' The boy nodded. 'Squadron mascots on recces. It went on, back in those days.' He caught the girl watching. *Fix a date, lad*! His thoughts strayed. 'A kite prangs in the forest – he could have jumped out and hopped it.'

'Loyal,' mused Rose, 'he'd go back. Maybe keep going back there.'

'It's an answer,' Steve ventured. He passed his cup and Di filled it. Fix the date and *then* tell her? He glanced at Tuck. There would be ructions. Heck, the flak would fly, Steve thought.

'Daft,' growled Tuck.

'But ingenious.' The girl put the pot down. 'It's a good explanation. What else does Zac go for? There's nothing else in those swamps besides the odd rusting aircraft. Steve, you're bright.' Her smile teased. 'Mind,' she told him, 'it's crazy!'

'Pass the sugar,' Rose ordered. 'You've not sweetened Steve's tea, girl.' The older woman leaned forward. 'He likes two, am I right, lad?'

'Well remembered.'

Rose smiled. She crooned softly. 'Another thing I remember: the first plane in the forest. No one knew where it crashed. Engines burning, they reckoned. Just a flame and then gone – like a comet, talk had it.'

'Talk!' Tuck scowled. He sat thinking. Luke had a nose for a plane wreck. 'Funny thing,' the man mumbled, 'that blamed dog hates Luke Wilson.'

Rose glanced up.

'Aye,' Di pondered. 'Sal says Luke knows the answer.'

'Sly bastard.'

'More cake, Steve?'

'Please,' said Steve. He ate stoutly. It beat the canteen confections, and he sat back feeling welcome, almost one of the household. He said, munching, 'It's a theory.'

'Huh,' said Tuck. But he added, 'Worth a word with the tinker. Luke's the man to get on to.'

'Dad!' snapped Di, her tone impatient.

'Tuck, she's told you,' Rose muttered, 'she's tried. He won't help. The man's nervous.'

'He's a right to be,' Tuck said.

'Dad, he won't talk, I've asked him.'

Tuck stretched. 'That's as maybe!' The brawny legs were thick-stockinged; boots left in the passage. He put his teacup down gently. Rose had set the best service. He steered his rough fist with caution. 'Time *I* paid Luke a visit. Time we knew where the dog was!'

He rammed his foot on the throttle. A pale sun swept the forest. It passed, fleetingly silver, chased on by the cloud-front. Tuck charged at the incline. Beyond the gunsite, he swerved, and stopped the truck on the heather. The clouds were drab, coldly mobile. He viewed the huts.

'Bloody Wilsons!'

Steve got down.

'Beggars,' Tuck said.

Steve grinned. Tuck was biased. Tom had been a good fellow. Steve followed the farmer, while ponies watched, scenting strangers. Tuck strode on, shoulders swinging. Motley fowl cleared a path and, as the two reached the dwellings, a child stared and vanished.

'Hey,' bawled Tuck, 'where's Luke Wilson?' He glared round at the rubbish. Some was burning, the smoke stinking. 'Hey, where's Luke?'

A door shifted. The child returned in Sal's clutches. He had his face to her neck, her arms cradling his bottom.

'Hello, Sal.' Steve was friendly. 'Seen Luke?'

She looked frightened.

'Come on, woman,' Tuck blustered.

Sal paused. Her glance darted. Flicking into the hut, it switched back to the men and ranged on to the chickens. For a moment, she hovered, then, child clinging, she was running, scattering the fowls.

'He's here.' Tuck stepped forward.

He pushed the door and Steve, advancing, perceived Luke's consternation. Surprised, the man shuffled backwards, his buttocks striking a table. A dead rabbit lay on it. There was a knife by the carcase. The hut was deeper in junk than when Benson had been there. Luke's hoard filled the corners but Tuck took little interest. He said, 'I want my dog, Wilson. You know where my dog is.'

'No.' Luke worked a hand backwards.

Tuck's fist struck the table. It swept the knife to the floor. 'B'God, you do,' snarled the farmer. He grabbed Luke by the collar. 'It's not the girl asking this time. This time, mister, you'll tell us.'

The man sprawled as Tuck shoved him. He wore, to Steve's deep resentment, an RAF flying-jacket. 'You'll mean the cur,' he said, flinching. 'It's the bog cur you're after?'

'*My* dog!'

'The stray mongrel.'

'Right,' said Tuck, 'the damned mongrel, the best dog I've had, Wilson.'

Steve had picked up a map-case. He saw a tail-wheel and compass. There were sections of perspex from a smashed cockpit window; part of an RAF roundel; sheets of bent and torn alloy, some with German paint on them. He quizzed the map. It bore vectors, the lines ruled in black crayon – the last flight calculations of an ill-fated airman.

He stared at Luke.

Tuck said, '*Where*, Luke?'

'I don't know where the dog is.'

'Bloody hell,' Steve said quietly, 'you scavenging liar.' He threw the map down, disgusted. 'You bloody bone-picking buzzard!'

'What d'you reckon?' Tuck asked him.

'He could cop it for this lot.'

'Fetch some lads from the gunsite.'

'No,' said Luke, 'I can help you. I *might* know.' Tuck stepped forward. 'He's not here,' whined Luke Wilson, 'the devil comes from the forest, haunts the swamps. I'd not go there ...'

'You've been!' Wilf Tuck grabbed him.

The man squirmed. 'And paid, gaffer! Not again ...'

'Aye, you'll take us.'

'Not for florins,' the man said. He tugged the leg of his trousers and Steve saw the tooth scars, angry bracelets, still raddled. Writhing free of the farmer, Luke slumped on his bedding. 'Not for you nor the Maker. I'd face the bench first and damn you. I'd keep my soul,' he asserted. 'You take yours to the devil – and take the air-gunner with you.'

Tuck turned to the rabbit; it was slit up the gut. Nearby on the table stood a small tin container. The farmer sniffed it, teeth clenched. 'Strychnine,' he said softly. 'By God, Steve, it's poison.'

He swung round on the tinker. The big man was fuming. 'Strychnine,' he said hoarsely. The farmer hauled the man

148

upright. 'You meant to poison him, damn you. You'd have poisoned the mongrel!'

Luke was choking. 'Get off me ...'

Tuck spluttered. 'I'll skin you!'

'Get him off me – do something.'

'Take it easy, boss,' Steve said.

'*Easy*, lad? He wants whipping! You seen a dog die of poisoning?'

Luke writhed. He was gasping, croaking. 'God help me, mister, the stuff's for rats, for the vermin!'

The farmer shook him. 'You're lying.' He pinned the man to the wall. 'Using rabbit for rat bait?' Tuck's voice was a whisper, a hissing indictment. 'You're bloody lying,' he shot. 'You were scheming to kill him, lay that filth for the mongrel. I should stuff your throat with it.'

Steve said, 'Boss ...'

'Let me be, lad.'

Luke's eyes popped. 'Wait – I'll do it. Christ in Heaven, I'll lead you! Far enough ...'

'To the dog, man.' Tuck drew back. 'Till we find him.' His face was grim. 'Or you'll rue it!'

He relaxed, and Luke hunched feebly.

Steve felt sick, claustrophobic. The hut was oppressive, filled with too many relics, tawdry trophies of death, the bric-à-brac of disaster. He said, 'The jacket, I'll take it.'

'It's mine.'

'Get it off, Luke!' The airman watched him. 'I'll mind it. Its owner's dead like your Tom is.'

Luke glared.

'Your own brother.'

The man removed the coat slowly. With a last wrench, he hurled it, not at Steve but at Tuck, diving suddenly past him, the big farmer blinded. Outside, Sal was gawping and they saw Luke's heels vanish. He ran like a whippet. Tuck swore. 'B'God, *next* time ...'

4

Steve started the Case. He let her throb for a minute then
took the spanners and tinkered. Report Luke – to what
purpose? Luke was only a tiddler. There were sharks with
gold fillings cashing in on war's horrors. The airman despised
them.

Di Tuck came through the farmyard. She was brisk. 'Did
you find him?'

Luke and more, he thought gravely. He pushed the fuel tap
and nodded, replacing a spanner. The engine died. 'Aye, he
hopped it.' He wiped his hands. 'Did a bunk,' he informed
her.

'Where's Dad?'

'Gone fence-making.'

'Steve' – she touched his arm quickly – 'the dog's been
seen. We might catch him.' She clucked her tongue. 'If you
hurry – if you leave that damned tractor!' She hustled him
from the lean-to. He saw the Jeep round the corner. 'This is
Greg,' she said briefly. Her smile challenged. 'I told you ...'

Steve looked blank.

'... in my letter.'

Greg said, 'Hi, Steve.' His clasp was friendly.

The airman stared. He was confused. She had in fact
mentioned something but Steve had taken scant notice. In
the flesh, Greg seemed daunting: assured, personable – Di's
sort.

'Our bull-tamer,' the girl coaxed.

What had Tuck said – *we'll lose her*? Steve said, 'Aye, you
did mention ...' Tuck had warned him, he reckoned. *Some
pen-pusher will thieve her. Or a Yank!* It made sense now.

The Yank grinned. 'You're Di's airman.'

'You're infantry?' Steve said.

Greg feigned gloom. 'Born unlucky. All she thinks of is

you, pal!' Di frowned and he added, 'You fixed up the day, Steve?'

'Greg ...' said Di.

'Day?' Steve gulped.

'Sure, the wedding.'

Steve liked him. He looked at Di. Her eyes cautioned, read his mind and were glinting. 'Oh, we've not ...' the girl started.

He clenched his fists. 'Next leave,' Steve said. The firmness surprised him.

She raised an eyebrow, unblinking. Poker-faced, she said tautly, 'Get in the Jeep, man, and listen – Greg's seen Zac by the forest. On the way here, he saw him.'

'Right,' drawled Greg. 'Couldn't miss him. At first he skirted the timbers then dived in among them. I'd know the spot. I could take you.'

Di said, 'We could track him.'

Steve was dazed, unbelieving. She had raised no objection. Next leave! Uncontested! His glance was smug, bright with triumph. He said, 'Track?' slightly tipsy. The boss had known his own daughter; there was a peck of Tuck in her. 'Track the mongrel?' Steve muttered.

'With another dog,' Greg said.

'Shep's bitch.' Di was eager. 'She's keen on the beggar. If we don't let the trail cool.'

'If Shep's willing,' Steve doubted.

As the Jeep rolled, Di whispered, 'You're a sly sod, you bastard. You pulled a fast one, God damn it!'

'Next leave!'

'You've a nerve, Steve.'

They stopped at the sheepfold and both dogs ran to greet them. Shep called them irately. He had a sack in his hands, and was filling troughs while he grumbled. The ewes jostled, and he cussed them. 'Brought the blamed forces wi' you,' he told the girl, looking past her. 'Ye'd think the war were a frolic.'

'Shep, they're helping me,' Di said.

'Helping, eh? Time you settled.' He sucked his pipe. 'Time you married.'

'So it seems.'

'Well?'

'We need you ...'

He heard her out with a grimace. Folding the sack, he surveyed her. 'Leave my sheep?' Shep said grimly. 'Go a-jaunting wi' that lot? I'd be fired.'

Di said, 'Rubbish. Dad wants the dog back. It's urgent.'

'More fool him.'

'We *all* want him.'

'Dog's footloose.'

'Oh, heavens, just bring the bitch and let's go, Shep!'

'To the forest?' He shuffled. Shep knocked his pipe on a hurdle. 'Dang the forest, young Dinah, that's no place for a woman. No damned place for a shepherd! You seen sheep in a forest? Maybe swine – not *these* creatures.'

The sheep were pushing for food, shoving long, wheeled troughs sideways. And starlings fed where they trampled, ducking under their noses. 'Lord,' wailed Di, 'there's a hurry.' She turned to Steve.

He said, 'Take her. Just take the bitch, we don't need him.'

Shep spat. 'Aye, and lose her.'

'On a line,' Di entreated. 'We'll keep the bitch on a line, Shep.'

He mouthed the empty pipe, brooding. At last, he croaked, 'Can't get baccy – can't find baccy now, nowheres.'

The young American watched them. A few miles off lay the Channel, the cold grey ride in his future. Europe's destiny tossed there. Now, the dog seemed more vital – and an old shepherd's humour. He tucked a hand in a pocket. 'D'you smoke sweet Virginian?' He passed his pouch and Shep sniffed it.

'Aye,' he wheezed, 'smells good, mister: smells like dog-hiring leaf, that.'

'Help yourself.'

'Keep the pouch?'

'While we use the bitch,' Greg said.

'Come *on*, Shep!'

'Done. Ye've got her.'

*

152

Zac looked round from the scrub. Away behind him lay Murton, the forge and Rutter's warning. Less removed, the gun swivelled, lean and black, its snout lofted. An air-raid siren had sounded, a faint wind-borne wailing, but the dog marched with purpose.

Ahead, the wood became forest. He moved alertly now, fox-like, as if infected with its wildness. Draughts stirred in the thickets. They seemed to raise stealthy spirits, the ghosts of villeins and bowmen, of verderers, outlaws. Zac stopped, as a shape loomed. He crept slowly forward, and it changed: at first human then a stunted grey ash bole.

The gnarled trunks cast illusions. Dark and twisted, they menaced, witnesses of past violence, of the bolt and the bludgeon, of stark blows in dim clearings. More than deer had been killed there. The ancient woods had been lawless. When kites spired and wolves foraged, the forest men had trod carefully.

Crouching low, the dog scurried. Above, the wind droned in branches, a whining hum like bees swarming. Old nests hung in bushes, wizened fetishes, crumbling, filled with the dregs of past seasons. And here and there in the brambles a leaf, pale side upwards, told where a hind's flank had brushed it.

There was a roar and Zac trembled.

A pair of Spitfires shot over, wing to wing, as if mated. Their noise chilled the mongrel. It pounded the forest and Zac, his ears flattened, lay prone as twigs scattered and a rotten branch crashed.

The roar had drubbed, growing louder ...

Zac had never forgotten. The sound of aircraft still frightened him and now, gulping saliva, the mongrel dog panted. Once more, he glanced backwards, perhaps seeking companions. Only trees met his vision, the underwood empty.

It was dusky, grey-shadowed, as he remembered the nightmare. At length, the sound grew fainter and he prowled on, his steps cautious. He knew the way from past visits. It led by brake-fern and birches, then by great lichened columns, through brush into thickets whose black wombs bred fungii.

Soon, the ground became soggy.

The dog paused, again listening.

And now, its engine resounding, a third plane swept over, trailing out of formation. Zac dived. The craft thundered. As it darkened the treetops, he froze in the earth, shaking, remembering all the horror.

The roar drubbed, growing louder, the plane plunging lower. An engine was flaming, tongues of fire trailing from it, fragmenting and glowing, each breath incandescent. The dog had found a recess, drawing back in the niche as the plane's pilot struggled.

The lad had laughed on the tarmac. 'We'll only be scouting.'

'We can't take the dog with us.'

'Can't?' The crew spoke in German.

'He won't like it.'

'He likes it less being left.' The flier hoisted the mongrel. 'Up you go, and keep mum. No word to our chiefs, Zac.'

'You'd think he was human.'

The other grinned. 'Don't insult him. Make a hash of those maps and you'll need his help getting home, friend!'

The bitch nosed round where the Jeep stopped then barked her excitement. Running back to the farm girl, the collie yelped and tugged the line Di was holding. 'Not much doubt he was here, Greg.'

They entered the forest. For a while, stepping freely – girl, soldier and airman, the shepherd's dog leading – they trod the lumber-scarred dragway once used by the woodmen. Here, in season, flowers blossomed: primrose, violets, bee orchis. Steve said, 'This is the good bit. It runs out at the clearing then the going gets tricky.' Already, brambles intruded, the underwood thickening.

Di said, 'Greg likes the forest; finds it friendly.' She stumbled. 'I think it's spooky, like Sal does.'

'It's kind of awesome,' Greg reckoned. 'It tries to speak to you – listen.' They heard the wind in the branches. The wood made primitive music. 'I guess it's telling us something; we're too cultured to grasp it.'

154

Di glanced at Steve. He grinned lewdly. 'Wait till your boots fill with bog, chum!'

'Hell,' the girl said, 'I'm tangled. Take the bitch, Steve, she's pulling.'

The sheepdog dived for a thicket. 'Oh no,' Steve restrained her, 'we're not fighting that lot!' He watched Di free her sweater. 'Scout around, Greg, we're nobbled.'

'Blast,' chafed Di, 'more time wasted!'

The soldier meandered. A sense of mystery wrapped him. The woods went back to pre-history. Stone Age men must have hid here, sheltering during winter with wild beasts and buzzards. What had they made, those rude hunters, of the forest and its secrets? He cast his eyes to a puddle. In the mud was a paw mark.

'Hey, this way!' They came running. 'There's a print; we're back on him!'

The collie bounded, and Steve scrambled after her.

Di drew breath. 'Good lass; seek, bitch!'

Now, they fought as the plane fell. Something sheered from the aircraft, spinning out into nowhere. Sparks were gushing, fumes streaming. From his funk-hole, the mongrel could see the craft's controls kicking, the pilot wrestling the column. The navigator was with him. Both were hauling, sweat-beaded, then the latter sprawled sideways, flung down as the plane lurched.

Zac smelled blood on a bulwark. The navigator rose, fumbling. As he rejoined the pilot, a perspex panel gleamed redly, reflecting the fireglow, the blaze from the motor.

The sun had beamed as they journeyed; it was welcome that winter. There had been casual banter and Zac, perched in the cockpit, had looked out on cloud anvils and watched racing propellers where the long wings vibrated. Wriggling up to his master, he had got his ears tickled. The pilot grinned as Zac's tail wagged.

'Anyone bring dog biscuits?'

The navigator's voice answered. 'I suppose the hound's driving!'

'Not yet, Willi, later.'

There was a groan. 'He believes it! He thinks that dog can do all things!'

'I'd not bet that he couldn't.'

Amused, the pilot sang quietly. Water sparkled beneath them, the plane's shadow small on it. 'Nobility, Zac is. His dam was a blue-blood.'

'Pull the other!'

'No joking.'

'Must have married beneath her.'

'An indiscretion . . .'

Di rested. 'Lord,' she said, 'how much farther?' The sheepdog was panting. Steve consulted his wristwatch; they had walked for an hour now. 'I hope she knows what she's doing. We could be going in circles.'

'Not unless the wind's shifted.' The American halted. 'She's held a pretty true bearing.'

'Still pulling,' Steve mumbled. 'We're in good and deep here.'

They pitched down a small chasm. It was mined by old diggings, generations of badgers, and the dog jumped fast water. It held no charm, dark and writhing, sluicing headlong beneath them. Sombre trees arched the fissure.

'Watch your step, the ground's sodden.'

The towering forest vault darkened.

'We're daft,' the girl grunted. Bizarre caves had embraced them, eerie evergreen arbours, the bowers closed to daylight, filled with dank exhalations. 'Your idea,' Steve responded. Their voices shrank in the timbers.

'Quite a spot,' Greg said, whistling.

'Weird,' breathed Di. 'I don't like it.' The bogs were close, the air heavy. Everywhere, dusk invaded, streaked with tendrils of swamp mist stealing in with sloth's fingers. They wreathed the trees, stalking the travellers. 'Steve!' The girl recoiled sharply, touched by shadowy ivy, its cold caress startling.

Now, their feet squelched, clod oozing, and where fallen wood mouldered great excrescences ripened. Di stopped by

the fungii. 'Steve!' She froze, saying, 'Listen ...' The
forest seemed to hush with them. The only sound was the
collie, her panting a tumult. 'Relax.' The men flanked the
farm girl.

'Easy,' Greg said, 'it's nothing.'

*Below, the Bofors had flashed and now mist swathed the
aircraft. It seemed to fly in jerks, blazing, lurching drunkenly
downwards. Zac was tight in his corner. The grey ground drew
closer.*

*Still, the pilot was fighting. As he ran out of airspace, the
burning craft shuddered, struck by something beneath it. Dark
fingers clawed upwards. Now, the trees were apparent, first a
few and then hundreds, their tops crowning the bog mist. All
around sprawled the forest.*

*There was a hammering impact. The plane slewed, bucked
and leapfrogged. Metal bore on the mongrel and, in the pounding
confusion, flames illumined great tree trunks. Torn, the ship
rushed on, screaming. A massive oak removed a wing. It
cartwheeled, fire streaming. Grinding, the fuselage skidded. The
dog was wedged in the cockpit. He knew no more for some
moments.*

*Then petrol was reeking. Half the cockpit had gone and the
creeping mist filled the rest. The burning engine was distant. Zac
jumped down into mud. He was dazed but intact and, looking
round for the others, saw the fuel ignite fiercely. Flames cocooned
the smashed cockpit.*

*Zac whimpered. His friends were still in the hulk and he tried
to get closer, but the searing heat beat him. Soon, ammunition
was crackling; spurts of fire, flying upwards, made plumes in the
vapour. Where their light pierced the fog, trees appeared, dim,
macabre.*

Steve sank to the ankle. He paused and raised his boot,
swearing. The mist hid the others. He saw the bitch stop and
look back, no longer pulling but cautious. She showed a
bristling excitement and Steve put his foot down.

'I think we're near,' he warned hoarsely.

Di and Greg loomed beside him. As the white vapour swirled, fleeting glimpses were offered of tufty swamp grasses. Open space marked the morass. Here and there the wood straggled, the trees growing whippy, engulfing the mire with necks of mean scrubland.

Di said tersely, 'Be careful.'

Greg exclaimed, 'Look – ahead, Steve!'

It climbed out of the murk, lank and bare, a lone ash pole. They stared up at its branches. A lump of metal was wedged there. No one spoke. Only the squelch when they moved, stepping warily forward, made any sound. The mist slithered.

From its coils rose small willows, a grid of wands, then more forest. Steve called quietly, 'An engine!' At first, it looked like a rock, partly covered by creeper. The propeller still jutted, the whole twisted and blackened, sinister in the herbage.

'One of *theirs*,' said the airman. He was a wraith in the mist and Di thought she misheard him. She could make out the soldier, and trees, and scattered wreckage. It was surreal in the vapour. Growth festooned chunks of alloy, gave life to rent metal.

She stopped. Di was fearful. Finding the Spitfire had chilled her: this plane was much larger. She did not wish to go on, to reach the core of destruction. Greg called. She went slowly.

'Jeez!' he said, an arm pointing.

The severed wing reared up hugely. Propped on end by a tree, it bore a black German cross, dark paint scorched, metal mangled. Di said, 'Wait ...' The tone shamed her. 'No, it's okay, I'm coming.' She braced, the murk thickening. Obscuring her escorts, it swirled as she shifted and advanced at last, her hands clammy.

A shrouded thorn rose before her. Groping, Di shuffled sideways. 'Steve?' She listened, eyes narrow. Shapes teased, slipped and glided. Limbs of great trees stretched dimly, seen then curtained from vision.

She seemed to hear, for one moment, a snarling threat, like

far thunder, then, she thought, the bitch fretting. Her pulse quick, the girl halted. She could sense something near her. It was inert, a dull presence – a presence Di knew she dreaded. She took a step. The mist parted.

'Di!' She heard Steve call sharply and at once saw the cockpit, side open, the crew there. Horror deluged on pity, sweeping close to hysteria. The girl held the tide back. What remained of the pilot, still in leather air-helmet, leaned towards her, his face gone.

She turned away, Steve's arms round her. Greg was holding the collie. 'Poor devils.' Steve nodded. The airman said, 'She's a Heinkel.'

A shadow stirred in the vapour. It seemed to issue from space, a slinking, watchful brute, growling. Di breathed, 'It's the mongrel.' His mane was stiff, the fangs menaced. 'Careful,' Steve warned, 'he's angry.'

'Protective,' the girl said.

'No wonder Luke won't return.'

'Zac!' The girl stepped towards him. 'Come on, Zac, don't be awkward.' The dog snarled, his lip curling. Then, inching forward, he snuffled. As he smelled them, he whimpered, sidling up, his tail twitching. The mongrel rolled while Di fussed him. 'You must be starving,' she blurted.

The men watched.

Di was moist-eyed. Shep's bitch nudged the mongrel. 'My God, he's thin!' The girl hugged him. 'You're coming home with us, damn you. You live with *us* now,' she scolded. He looked round sadly. 'Poor mongrel ...'

'Di' – the Yank touched her shoulder – 'this is no place to linger.'

'Aye,' said Steve, 'come away, Di.'

'You too, dog. The boss needs you.'

They walked a short way and halted. Looking back, Zac beside them, they saw the wreck in the vapour. Di Tuck stroked the mongrel. 'They're at peace,' the girl told him. 'No one's going to disturb them.'

159

5

They were married in winter. The cold grey church was unheated and outside, where sheep huddled, jackdaws fought a nor'wester. In the rawness, Rose shivered. 'Reckon,' Tuck said, 'they're suited,' to which she answered, 'They're in love.'

'Fair start, Rosie.'

'Fair?' said Rose. Her lip trembled. 'Rations, bombs, separation?'

'They'll have the farm.'

'One day – maybe.'

Di and Steve left for London: two nights, Steve's pass limit. They strolled a while in the black-out, glimpsed St Paul's by the searchlights, enjoyed some Crazy Gang slapstick. For the rest, they stayed in, feeding coins to a meter to keep a glow in the gasfire they watched from their pillow.

Back at home, Zac was waiting. 'Zac, I'm mad,' the girl whispered. Her eyes were sad, full of love still. Were *they* mad where Zac came from? Did *their* girls marry airmen? 'I must be dotty,' Steve's bride said.

The mongrel consoled her. He had looked his age lately, she thought – four years now in England, perhaps a third of a lifetime. The dog was white-faced, his eyes rheumy. And growing deaf, the girl reckoned.

True, he still went off sometimes, though the absences shortened. Few spoke of Zac's secret. Murton, never forthcoming, respected the mongrel, tight-lipped towards strangers. 'It's no damned business of others,' said Rutter, his brow drawn. 'That's a good old dog – damn 'em!'

'He'll not give up,' Tuck predicted. They were threshing, Zac eager. 'He'll be in with those rats, Rose.'

'Just take care of him,' Rose said. They stood by the

engine. 'That corn rick's infested. Don't let the dog overdo it.'

'Go on,' Tuck said, 'I'll watch him.'

She walked away with her buckets. The thresher drummed, Di bond-cutting, standing in for Luke Wilson. 'Luke?' The threshing boss snickered. 'You'd not drag Luke *here* with horses!'

'I'd not have him here, mister.'

'It's the mongrel. They reckon ...'

'Aye,' said Tuck, 'let 'em reckon. I pay for work not for reckoning!'

'Rum old dog.'

'You could say so.'

Rose paused. She watched Dinah. Brown dust billowed round her as the great engine shook. Men tossed sheaves to the farm girl. Her face was grimed; the knife glinted. It was no life, thought her mother, away from a husband, half afraid of the postman. If the war could be over ...

Rose moved on, buckets dragging. If they could land back in Europe, get the 'second front' open ...

Even that prospect frightened. Di, she knew, dreaded summer, the promised Allied invasion. Only Jim, young and sanguine, viewed *that* day without horrors. 'Mrs Tuck, I could be there – if they wait,' he had told her. 'Heck, I'd show 'em, for Roy's sake!'

'Would you, Jim?' Her mouth hardened. 'Damn it, boy, that talk's stupid.'

'Don't see why.'

'Some might tell you – some with husbands to lose, lad. Don't you let the girl hear you.'

Jim worked now at the engine. Stooping under the thresher, he raked the dust, his eyes smarting. Chaff and cavings engulfed him. They filled his shirt, ringed his collar. 'Keep it up, son,' Tuck bellowed. Jim grinned. He liked threshing. The noise and bustle were thrilling, the filth a minor objection.

'We'll be back, boss, this summer.'

'Back?' Tuck shifted a corn bag.

Jim glanced at Di. The drums thundered. There was no chance she could hear him. 'In France, boss, the invasion. There's troops all over, a-waiting. Another year, *I* could be there.'

'Huh!' said Tuck.

'Steve'll show 'em. First in, towing the gliders! I'd volunteer ...'

'Just keep raking!' Zac barked and Tuck shouted, 'I'll be damned, see *that* beggar?' A rat had left the rick early. It beat the dog to the buildings. 'Less talk, boy, fetch the hen-wire. We'll stop 'em escaping.'

Tuck eyed the threshing contractor. The man leered. 'One gone, master.' He checked the strap. 'And a big 'un. The dog should have had him.'

'He'll have them!' Tuck smouldered. Jim was wiring the corn stack. 'You wait,' said the farmer, 'he'll have them. When they get to the bottom. That's a ratting dog, mister.'

Head on paws, the dog rested. His snout was grey, his eyes hooded. The stack lost height as the sheaves flew. 'By hell,' the pitchers were calling, 'there's some livestock in this 'un!'

'Stood o'er long.'

'Rats are swarming!'

The farmer beckoned the mongrel. They were down to the sticks and, when the men moved the bundles, a glimpse of seething life met them. 'Go on, dog, seize the beggars!' The thresher's roar had subsided. In the stillness that followed, the squeal of rodents was awesome.

'There's three-score of 'em, master!'

Zac was swirling and snapping. As he lunged, rats leeched to him, the old dog's teeth crackling. Tuck grabbed a fork, wading forward. He stood beside the dog, stabbing. The men were prodding and kicking, knocking rats from their leggings.

Enraged, the mongrel dog battled, his lips torn and ears bleeding. The rodents spun as he tossed them, then, pouncing, shook others. They fell on top of each other, grey-brown monsters, corn-bloated.

'Easy, Zac.' Tuck grew worried. The old dog was frenzied.

Still he toiled, digging, rooting, rummaging under faggots. At last, his strength left him. He swung one more brown vandal then staggered, his eyes glazing. 'Zac!' bawled Tuck.

'Boss,' cried Jim, 'he's collapsed, boss!'

'Fetch some water,' Tuck told him. The farmer knelt by the mongrel. Di was down from the thresher. 'The old fool,' said her father. 'He wouldn't give over. I called.'

'He's deaf,' Di said.

'Let him drink; he's exhausted.' The dog licked Jim's fingers. They were wet from the yard trough. Tuck lifted the mongrel.

He carried Zac to the farmhouse.

'Lord,' screeched Rose, 'and I warned you!'

'He wouldn't stop ...'

'By the fire, Wilf, on the rug. Zac, you lie there!'

'He'll perk up.'

'The *bites* on him!'

'Daft old fool ...'

'Tuck, I warned you.'

'He must have killed near two dozen.' Jim considered the mongrel. The dog was curled in the sun as they mucked out the bull-pen – the beast again in the meadow – and Jim said like a veteran, 'I never seen nothing like it.'

'Near killed *himself*,' said the farmer. The dog had slowly recovered. Now, he watched as they laboured, heaving muck to the tip-cart.

Each forkful was taxing. The steaming compound strained muscles, tightened fists so the bone showed. Tuck's smooth rhythm was practised; the burly Jim sweated. He said, 'Next birthday, they'll have me. I'll try for the Airborne.'

Tuck slung muck. He said roughly, 'You've as much chance as *that* has!'

Jim frowned. His mind struggled. 'I dun'no ...' he mused dourly. At length, he said, 'Well, the Hampshires. I allus lived here – they'd take me.'

'Bah, you'd go where they put you: likely, scrubbing latrines, lad.' Tuck barked, then, less harshly – he had lost

Roy to the army and did not mean to let Jim go, for the farm's sake and Jim's sake – 'The war won't miss you but I would. We *all* would, you belong here.'

The man paused, his fork rested. He went on, 'You'd miss Murton, the farm and surroundings.' His gaze sought the landscape. Once in a while, Tuck looked round him, his mind detached from the farm chores, the raw facts of his calling, and dwelled on the distant downland, cloud-shadowed; the purple fastness of forest; greens that glowed like a cat's eye.

'By thunder, you'd miss it!'

'Miss the muck?' Jim said slyly.

The man heaved straw and dung upwards. Its weight made the cart jolt. 'Puts strength in you,' Tuck said. 'Into you and the land, boy. The breath o' muck renews vigour.'

'They say muck won't be needed – in time to come.'

'They *do*, do they?'

Jim rubbed a wrist on his forehead. 'So I heard,' the lad answered. 'They say the soil won't be rested; we'll take corn every year from the same land, no mucking. All by chemicals, some say.'

'Not while I'm here,' the man said.

'It's what I heard.'

Di approached them. Her sturdy grace raised Tuck's spirits. The farmer trusted her judgement. 'Bang his head, girl, he's rambling! Farming's giving and taking – take what's fair but put back, lad.'

Di quizzed them. 'A sermon?'

Tuck spat. 'And well needed. There's generations unborn yet.'

'Come on, Dad, it's not Sunday!'

'You take heed ...'

The girl stopped him. 'Brindle's calved; it's a heifer.'

'Another heifer?' Tuck brightened. 'Good old beast. You'd best fetch them. And take Jim; you know Brindle ...'

'Bloody *do*!' The girl chuckled.

She turned and he squinted, watching Di's robust movements, the flowing harmony of them, hips as smooth as a sow's flanks. He thought they just might have thickened.

'Have a care.' Tuck looked thoughtful. He was set on a grandson. 'Go on, Jim. I'll clear this lot.'

Steve's wife drove the Fergy. Jim, behind with the farm dog, said, 'I'd reckoned on Airborne.'

Di's voice whipped. 'What's he told you?'

'That I should stay on the farm.'

'You've a while to go yet, Jim.' She glanced back at the trailer. Tuck, she thought, was right this time: Jim needed dissuading. He was not like Steve – Jim was childlike. The trailer bumped. 'Think it over.' Her hair streamed. 'There's no hurry. Let's see later,' the girl said.

The sky had filled and was drizzling.

'Greg's in infantry,' Jim said.

'Yes.'

'They'll land on the beaches ...' He checked himself, remembering Rose.

Di swung the wheel. 'Jim,' she shouted. 'Farming's just as important. Feeding people, for God's sake. Never mind Steve and Greg, the farm needs you. *I* need you.' They passed the bull, tractor bouncing. 'You're a boon.'

The bull watched them. Idly rubbing a paling, the great animal paused, a threatening eye on the mongrel. Zac growled from the trailer. Jim, relieved to pass quickly, for the bull scared the farm lad, held the dog by the collar. The hulking beast fell behind them.

On they rattled, Zac swaying. Jim placed an arm round the mongrel. 'Will he ever go home now?'

'Zac?' Di smiled. 'Jim, how *could* he?'

'When the war's done.'

'You blockhead! How'd we find his home, damn it? Besides, he'll not see the war out. The old beggar's near finished.'

'Must have come from a farm, once.'

'Maybe, Jim.' Di was silent.

They grew damp the rain clinging. Moisture heightened the hedge smells, scents of grass, shrub and herbage the girl found nostalgic, like cow-parsley in spring and the sweet, creamy mayflowers. Her childhood haunted the farm lanes –

165

hers and Roy's. The rain drifted.

'Odd,' mused Jim. 'Zac's an odd 'un – loyal to both sides. Odd, that is ...'

'He's just a dog, Jim.'

'I reckon.' Kind of simple, Jim reasoned; not the brains to make war or bomb people, or suchlike.

'There she is!' Di braked smoothly. 'There's our calf – swing the gate, Jim.'

Brindle lowed. The bull answered. In the mizzle, its coat shone. Dampness slicked the vast shoulders. Massively, the beast fretted, slowly budging the fence-post. The wire loosened, the slack hidden by brambles which the bull nosed.

Its roar blared.

6

The dog limped to the warren. At the coombe's lip, he rested. Movement was a problem now. His hips were bad. Walking was awkward, and when he ran – which was seldom – the mongrel rocked like a seesaw, all the power in his forelegs.

Stubbornly, the dog coped. Indeed, he made little fuss, complaining more of his deafness, barking gruffly at nothing as if scolding the silence, though he seemed to hear some things. He cocked an ear as lambs bleated and, now, at the cuckoo.

But he missed the dull thunder. For many days it had sounded, the steady rumble of convoys – lorries, Jeeps, Bren-gun-carriers – passing coastwards, troop-laden.

Zac wormed down by the sheep path. Rabbits browsed in the coombe, but the dog did not try to chase them. Instead, where the gorse grew, he waited, his nose to the breeze.

Abruptly, Shep's bitch burst forward. She almost dived down the bank and he greeted her gamely on his toes as she skittered. The female danced, pleased to see him, then they sprawled, their tongues lolling.

Shep whistled.

They idled.

'Come on back, bitch. Where are you?'

The air was still. Tanks were rolling.

'If that dog's there, I'll baste him. I've had enough of the mongrel!'

The sheepdog stirred. Zac rose stiffly. As she left, his eyes followed wistfully where the bitch bounded. He took a slow stride and staggered. Alone again, he stood snuffling then dragged himself into Murton.

'Blamed old dog,' said the farmer. Tuck was speaking to Rutter. The smith was shoeing the ploughteam. 'He's not safe in this traffic.' The army convoys seemed endless. They shook the forge as they passed, grinding down to the Channel, and Tuck soothed the horses. 'He'll get killed.'

'He's not dim, Wilf.'

Tuck saw Zac sway towards them. 'Deaf!' he groaned, eyes averted. Tank treads squealed and men shouted. A Sherman slewed, ripping turf, then swerved back on course with a lurch. Engines roared; horses whinnied. Zac strolled into the blacksmith's.

Rutter cackled. 'He's lucky.' Lorries revved, changing gear, and he said, 'His luck's famous. A fellow called asking questions ...'

Sherman tanks rocked the village. Tuck's youngest gelding was fretting and Zac sat beside him. The old dog calmed the horses.

'Questions?' Tuck said.

'Word travels.' Rutter bent to the anvil. 'Can't prevent gossip spreading.'

'*What* fellow?'

'Official.' The blacksmith straightened. 'A snooper. Suit and briefcase.' He hammered. The sparks jumped and he muttered, 'Stiff hat and fool questions – like, had a stray dog been kept here, a dog we couldn't account for.' Rutter leered. 'Regulations – to do with livestock importing.'

'Whoa, now!' Tuck fussed his ploughsteeds. 'Damn the gossip,' he blathered.

'Oh, don't worry,' the smith said, 'he must have got the wrong village. Could be Burton, I told him, near Christchurch. Not *Murton*. I sent him off down by Bransgore. With luck, he ran out of petrol. The dog's *our* business – blamed snoopers!'

'Mr Tuck!' A Jeep shunted. The men saw four lads in helmets.

Zac looked up, his jaws grinding. The dog still relished hoof parings.

'Greg?' Tuck peered.

'Right you are, sir!' The driver shoved back his headgear and smiled. 'Saw the mongrel.'

'I'll be damned!'

'Couldn't miss him!'

The farmer grinned. 'Are you fit, son?' He eyed their guns and said, frowning, 'Moving out soon, I reckon.' An army motorbike halted and its rider spread a map.

A corporal said, 'It's the big one.'

'How's Di?'

'She got married.'

'They always do,' Greg lamented, 'the ones I fall for, God damn it! Nice guy, Steve, hope he makes it.' Time was short. 'Say you met me.' He called to Zac, who came forward, face creased, his tail wagging. 'Still not parting?' the Yank said. 'We could give him a lift, sir.'

'He's retired.'

'Then we'll take him.'

'The hell you will!'

Zac barked deeply. As the Jeep rolled, Greg muttered, 'Mr Tuck, take things easy ...'

'You, too, lad,' said the farmer.

'Wish I'd seen Greg,' Di murmured.

'They hardly stopped,' her father told her. He found his glasses and cleaned them. Tuck wore glasses for reading, perched down by his nostrils. They looked incongruous on him, with the breeches and braces, open shirt, craggy features. He read the paper, now lunch was over.

'It could've been the last chance, Dad.'

Rose piled plates. 'Shouldn't think so.'

'Ma, they'll cross any day now.'

'Aye.' He scanned the headlines. 'The coast's stiff with soldiers.'

Rose frowned.

Di looked strained. They piled the crocks in the kitchen. She almost trod on the mongrel. Any day, the girl reckoned, and the gliders would head them. 'Steve's not phoned.' Her voice faltered. She felt sick. Flies were buzzing. They were thick by the sink and Steve's wife, seldom squeamish, was suddenly queasy. She braced.

'You all right, Di?'

The girl nodded. 'It's waiting.'

Tuck said slowly, 'He'll call you.' He looked up. 'Always has done.'

'Can't you phone the mess?' Rose asked.

'No chance: they won't have it. I've a number he gave me.' It was the pub the crew haunted. 'Don't suppose he'll be in, though.'

'Try it, lass.'

Their own phone rang.

Di jumped. Both were startled. '*There*,' laughed Rose, 'someone heard us!' She paused. 'Pick it up, then!'

It seemed to Di a great effort.

'Hello?'

The line crackled.

'Dinah?' queried Doc Benson.

Her shoulders slumped as Benson waffled. She did not need the man's lecture. Rose and Sal had convinced her she was pregnant, Sal with daunting persuasion. 'It's writ all over you, lady. Test?' Sal's glance had been scornful. 'Would I lie, heaven strike me?'

Di guessed not. Sal's child mocked her, born the son of a dead man. It was *Steve* the girl wanted, not his fatherless offspring.

She put the phone down. Di gritted, 'Test was positive.'

'Bless you!'

She felt numb as Rose hugged her. Tuck peered over his glasses. 'Good for Steve, that'll please him!' It pleased the farmer, his face said.

Di went out, the dog with her. In the yard, Zac kept close, his nose nudging her fingers. Strange, she thought, how he knew; how a dog sensed emotion, picked up fear, sadness, mischief, with infallible instinct. Poor old Zac. 'Zac, I need him!'

She beat a fist on the Case, her body pressed to the engine. Steve loved the contraption. She could see him now driving, riding up on the ploughswell, clouds rolling, gulls flocking.

'I *need* him, dog!' Her eyes scalded. She saw Steve in the warren, in the fleapit, in London. He had bought her violets

170

in London, the bunch costing sixpence – violets *free* all her girlhood! Steve reckoned Luke had picked them!

'Miss ...'

Jim ran from the lane.

The girl started, her cheeks damp, still 'miss' to the farm lad who said, puffing, 'He's vanished. I just come by and he's vanished!'

'Jim?' She cursed him, her face turned.

'You beware, miss; be watchful.'

'Now, Jim ...' Her chin lifted. She brushed an eye. 'What's the trouble?'

'I come by – he was gone.' The lad was red-faced, eyes rolling. 'Best be ready to hop it.'

'Jim, calm down.' Steve's wife straightened.

'He's been queer, sort of restless.'

She stepped away from the tractor. The sky was churning with clouds: the kind of clouds Steve would speak of, roofed with sun when you climbed them, flew over their summits. 'Hold on,' Di said, 'you're babbling. Start again – tell me slowly.'

Jim looked over his shoulder. The dog was scratching. 'He's vanished. I come by and the bull's gone. He's broke the fence.'

'Are you *certain*?'

'You can see where he's trampled.' The youth turned nervously, adding, 'Across the verge to the road. He's on the loose; you beware, miss.'

Di scanned the lane. 'It's all right, Jim.' The crowding cloud-shadows scurried. 'I'll tell the boss. Where's the cowman?'

'Likely still at his cottage.'

'You'd better find him and warn him.'

Di returned to the farmhouse. Tuck was leaving and Rose said, 'Well, it's finally happening. The whole of Murton has told you; now at last, Tuck, you'll listen. The brute's had a brainstorm – it had *you* down, now it's footloose, most probably raging.'

'Don't be daft.'

'Mauling someone.'

'Huh!' he said but he told her, 'Phone the constable, woman. I'll get out the Morris. He'll not be far. Where's the boy, Di?'

'Gone down to the cowman.'

'Shep won't know – I'd best tell him.'

'I'll come,' Di said.

'You'll stay here!'

'She *will*,' Rose said. 'You get on with it, damn you, I'll mind *her*.'

'Ma . . .'

'Show sense, girl!'

Tuck drove off past the mongrel. 'Stay there, Zac, you'll be safer.' The dog barked, affronted. He took a couple of paces and stopped, his sinew feeble, but his eyes were fierce on the Morris. As it left, he sat watching and howled his resentment.

Tuck put his foot down. He wished Zac was still strong – he would have liked the dog with him. There was no sign of the bull. He hoped Jim had been wrong, but when he braked near the fence he could see it was down, and he charged on, his shirt sticky.

If the creature reached Murton . . .

The farmer peered as the truck raced. The lane ahead was deserted; a shadowed land, peaceful. Too peaceful, Tuck reckoned; he should have spotted his quarry. He hurled the truck past the warren and round the bend. Still no shorthorn.

Tuck jumped down where the sheep browsed. 'Shep!' The fellow was missing. Tuck shouted, advancing. 'Shepherd, damn you!' he bellowed, 'I've no time for traipsing!' He reached the wheeled hut, his breath short.

'In a hurry?' Shep mumbled.

He was hunched on the lee-side, where the steps were, his mouth full. Looking up, he drank slowly, swigging tea from a bottle, an old sock pulled round it.

'Blast it, shepherd, time's precious!'

'Aye,' said Shep, 'so's my lunch-break.'

He looked, thought Tuck, like a ragbag, a parcel of sacking.

172

The farmer's eye scanned the hollow. 'You'd best watch out, the bull's missing. By chance, you've not seen the beggar?'

'Lost a bull?' Shep's glance darted. He wiped the mouth of the bottle. 'Fair-sized creature,' he taunted.

'Well?' snarled Tuck.

'Might of seen him ...'

'In the lane?'

'So I reckon.'

'Bound for Murton?'

'Wrong, master.' Tuck's relief was abortive. 'Or I'd not be sat lunching. The beast was bound for the dairy. The cowman'll seize him.'

Cowman! Tuck revved the Morris. The bull would mangle the fellow. A damned old fool, like the shepherd. They were a pair and both senile!

7

Tuck punished the lorry. The engine bearings were rattling. He thought the lot might blow up but he drove like the devil, a great dread descending, overwhelming all prudence. He thought an axle would crack, that the driveshaft would shatter.

In his fists, the wheel wrestled, twisting wildly at corners, whipping back as tyres blistered. He dared not dwell on his fear – his concern for the cowman – but it grew as he drove, now more real than his onrush, than the shades in the windscreen.

Hedge and field fled like shadows, woods and cottages flitted. As he roared past Ten Acre, the dairy loomed vaguely, filling shuddering glass until, suddenly halting, Tuck faced his fear's image.

The man lay on the verge, his crippled leg sticking out stiffly. At his back was the wall. Jim had scrambled across it wall and was screaming and waving, hurling grit at the shorthorn. The beast blocked the roadway. It had its head down, eyes level, gaze fixed on the cowman.

'Don't move!' bawled the farmer.

Rose had said, 'He'll kill someone.' Tuck's wife loathed the monster. 'One day, Wilf, he'll kill someone and on your head be it!'

He took a stick from the lorry.

The cowman's eyes watched him. They were oddly impassive. For once, the man's face lacked rancour, seemed kinder, less twisted. The man had not always suffered. Tuck had known him to whistle, and shake the byre with his laughter. He had grown bitter with age, yet, in peril, looked calmer; resigned, thought the farmer.

Jim was gawping, an arm raised.

'Keep still,' rapped the big man.

Tensely, Tuck shifted closer. He held the stick out, crook forward. He could have touched the bull's flank but his aim was the head, to slip the stick through the nose-ring. 'Whoa,' he croaked, 'steady, damn you!' He stretched. 'Whoa, beast – steady!' He saw Jim still frozen, mouth wide, then the bull heaved.

It came round, its tail lashing, tumbling Tuck like a ninepin. He hit the wall. The bull rushed him. Dazed, he flailed his stick at it and saw the beast change direction, drawn again to the cowman.

Jim had hurdled the stonework. Stooping to the cripple, he was trying to raise him as the beast put its horns down. 'Leave him, boy!' Tuck lurched forward. 'Get back, I'll stay with him ...'

The bull was scraping, tail swishing. Tuck choked as the dust flew. 'Mad sod,' coughed the cowman.

'Don't move,' said the farmer.

He inched sideways, his arms spread. Stick flicking, he waited, eyes drilling the monster. It came deceptively slowly, a ton weight, shoulders rolling, and its owner, bowled backwards, saw the great head above him. Jim bawled. Tuck was sprawling. He had no chance, thought the farm lad.

He heard a growl through the dust.

The dog crouched in the roadway. His tongue lolled, his legs quivered. Zac was breathless from walking, his limbs weak, but he snarled and the bull, turning, snorted.

Old foes, they stood glowering. Zac remembered their scrimmage; the bull, the dog's taunting. Then the moment was broken.

Tuck saw the bull charge the mongrel. The old dog could not dodge. He had one place of safety – beneath the monster's neck – and, grabbing its dewlap, Zac clung with tenacious jaws.

Enraged, the bull swung him. Zac held on. Tuck was rising, watching Jim scramble forward, again with the cowman. Still Zac leeched to the shorthorn, dragged now to a gate, where the bull tried to crush him. 'Come off, Zac!' Tuck was swaying, groping back to the Morris. Through the gate lay the cowyard. He started the motor.

Tuck saw the bull through the windscreen. The lorry was moving. He saw a great flank draw closer. He prayed the dog would fall clear, then felt a bump. The bull bellowed. Forced to the yard, it was trapped; the truck was jammed in the exit.

Tuck got down. 'You hurt, cowman?'

'I'm one piece. Where's the mongrel?'

Zac was under the lorry.

'Come on out, dog,' Tuck pleaded. He knelt by the tailboard. He could see a grey muzzle. Zac appeared, and the farmer held him.

'He's whacked,' said Jim.

'He's safe,' Tuck said.

A car stopped and Rose burst from it. 'You're alive!' She glared round her. Jim blinked. 'The great bumpkin! No thanks to him that you're living! I hope you're pleased, Tuck, with this – that you've scared the wits from us?'

Benson stepped from the Vauxhall.

'All but killed!' cried the woman.

'Zac was here,' Jim said gravely.

'Poor old devil,' Rose countered. 'What'll Tuck do without him? Poor old Zac – the dog's dying and you still need the beggar!'

'Well,' said Benson, 'who's damaged?'

Tuck scowled. 'Check the cowman.'

'Damn that,' said the cripple, 'I don't need a doctor!' He looked at Rose, his glance pointed. 'All we need is the knacker.'

'Aye,' said Rose, 'the bull's going.'

Tuck led the bull to the gate. The beast was mild as a lamb and licked its nose, shuffling meekly. 'If he was always like this, Wilf!' The slaughterer squinted. 'He'd run amok if we trucked him.'

'I don't know,' Tuck said grimly.

'Safer here, though, I reckon.'

The farmer said, 'He's not evil. Daft at times but not *evil*.'

'Done you well?'

'He has, damn him!' Tuck slapped the beast, his jaw tightening. 'It's a crime ...'

'It's luck, gaffer.' The knacker took out a cartridge. 'Once they've turned, you can't trust them.' He primed the slayer. 'Too risky – b'God, your girl's on the farm, Wilf; you can't risk your daughter.'

Or a grandson, Tuck brooded.

The knacker lifted the tool. The metal touched the bull's forehead, where the hair was white and crinkly, as curled as a toddler's. At least, thought Tuck, his fists clenching, the beast had not smelled a death-house or had to wait at the knacker's. He heard the thud of the cartridge.

Tuck put a mask on his anguish. 'He wasn't *bad*. Frightened people ...' Their fear had made the bull awkward.

The yard was quiet, the sun shining. The beast stood up for a moment then dropped as if boneless, falling slowly, weight sagging. Stretched out, it seemed vaster, the corpse monumental, the sky blue in one eyeball, the earthy hooves massive. It was a force wasted, Tuck thought, a sin – like Roy's slaughter.

He helped the man with the tackle. They winched the beast on the loader. 'I'll send a cheque,' growled the knacker. He knew how Tuck felt. 'Be *something* ...'

Tuck nodded.

He walked away and Zac followed. 'Come on, dog.' Dinah joined them. She had come from the stable and took the big man's arm fondly. 'Never mind ...'

'It's a crime, lass.'

'We'll be safer,' the girl said. 'Ma's been worried too long, Tuck.'

'I suppose.'

'Buy a young one.' They stopped where heifers were grazing, echoing the bull's markings. The creatures saw them and gambolled. 'Do no harm, some new blood, Dad.'

'Daresay ...'

The dog rested. Zac chose the shade, his head lowered, his gaze on the farmer. Movement wearied the mongrel. Rose shrilled and his ears cocked. Even Zac heard Rose calling. 'Di!' she screeched. 'It's the phone, Di!'

'Go on,' Tuck said.

She sprinted. At the door, Rose was waiting. 'It's Steve – catch your breath, girl!' Di gulped. She barged forward and snatched the phone. 'Steve?' she blurted.

'You're panting,' his voice said.

Tuck came in.

'Ran,' she gabbled.

Steve laughed.

'You're safe,' Di said.

Tuck went through to the parlour.

'Safe?' said Steve. 'Nothing's started.'

'Yes, it has, Steve.'

'The landings?'

'No.'

'Then what?'

'Do you love me?'

'Depends!'

'Steve, I'm pregnant.' Di paused. 'Are you sorry?'

'*Sorry?*' Steve gasped.

'I wondered.'

'Bloody hell, it's a knockout! It's brilliant! There'll be a booze-up this evening ...' He hesitated. '*You're* glad, Di?'

'Steve, I love you ...'

'Yes – listen.' He tried to make it sound casual. 'Leave's cancelled. There's a bit of a fuss on, passes stopped, preparations. You can guess. Di, don't worry. Soon be done then I'll see you. We'll celebrate the good news, Di.'

Rose said later, 'He's right, don't you worry. Just you keep good and healthy.'

'He'll be home,' said the farmer. 'He's not like Greg, who'll be landing: with Steve the job's there and back, drop the lads and return. Once it's done, he'll be with us.'

Benson, there for eggs, grunted.

Rose said, '*You* tell her, Doctor, she needs to keep cheerful.'

'She's a wise girl,' said Benson. He changed tack. 'Has the bull gone?'

Rose said, 'Yes,' and as briskly, 'Wilf, we've still got some whisky. The doctor would like some.'

'Then he'd best have it,' Tuck snarled. They only kept it for Benson! He said thickly, 'The bull's gone. You can drink to that, mister!'

'Tuck's done right.' Rose stood by him. 'It was hard but it's over.' She stooped, fondling the farm dog. 'Now the old mongrel's slipping.'

'Yes,' said Di, 'tell us, Doctor ...'

Benson drained his glass, coughing. He eyed the bottle. 'His heart's weak.' He felt Zac's pulse. 'Not much left.'

'He's been dizzy,' Rose told him.

Tuck filled the glass. 'Can we treat him?'

'Ask the vet.' Benson tippled. 'You could try digitalis – pump more blood where it's needed – but the dog's done well, Wilfred. He's worn out.'

The dog watched them. Di embraced him and his tail thumped.

Jackdaws soared over Murton, wings dark as the cloud hills. With dusky skies came a tension, concern for hay and invasion, for provision and venture. Villagers stood in doorways, sat by wirelesses, waiting.

Slowly, Zac climbed the incline. Each step was exhausting. At times, the mongrel would stagger, going down on his chin, but he heaved himself forward. His neck was stiff, his will dogged. On the ridge, he stood panting and cast his gaze backwards.

By the house, great trees billowed. Jim had bicycled home but the girl was still busy, now watering horses at the trough near the stables. The creatures peered, dribbling.

Rose was gathering washing. Arms raised to the clothes-line, she fought with sheets, her hair ruffled. Cows disgorged from the dairy. Countless times, Zac had steered them. Now they idled, day-dreaming, straggling out to the pasture.

The evening scene was familiar: shadowed lane, dung-encrusted; the dusty rickyard and grain barn; the shed where the Case stood. Soon the farm cats would prowl and a far searchlight flicker.

He could still see a tractor. Tuck was working late, spinning, turning hay in the distance, and Zac's deaf ears flattened. His old eyes ran with mucus. Thus, he stood a while longer, then, sighing, hauled onwards.

The sun was low when Tuck missed him.

At first, the man searched the hedge where his jacket lay folded. Zac would wait in the hedgerow. Later, Tuck asked his daughter. 'Maybe,' Di said, 'he's home,' but Rose Tuck had not seen him.

'Not since Jim brought the milk.'

'He'd not have followed Jim, would he?'

'Never has,' Rose reflected. Zac had looked frail that morning, scarcely stirring at breakfast, still around after lunch. Once, the dog had come to her, his low whimper affecting, and Rose had stopped her egg-scrubbing to comfort the mongrel. She should have spared him more time, she knew now – instinct told her, an intuitive feeling.

'He's gone,' she said. 'Gone for good, Tuck.'

'Gone?' the girl said.

'Forever.'

'Aye,' said Tuck, his face troubled, 'I've known them wander off quietly.' He saw the girl's dismay rising. 'Come on,' he told her, 'look lively. We'll ask Jim.'

'He's left,' Rose said.

'Catch him home.'

Dinah followed.

The sky was patchy, unsettled. Tuck glanced at the rain clouds. 'June the third,' the man muttered, 'I'd bargained for better.'

'Damn the weather – light's going.'

They reached the village in silence. It was dusk and a shower was starting. Jim and Rutter stood watching, sheltered where the forge roofed them, the blacksmith's pipe fiery. 'Jim,' Tuck hailed from the lorry, 'you seen the old mongrel?'

Jim's head shook.

'He's pushed off, lad.'

'I've not seen him.' Jim pondered. 'Not tonight.'

A bat flitted. Rutter sucked and the pipe glowed. He said, 'You know where he'll head for – he'll be bound for that forest.'

'Never make it,' Tuck answered.

'You'd be surprised.'

'The dog's dying.'

'I'd say he'll die where he wants to.'

'Go on, Dad' – Di sat forward – 'try the heath while there's time. We won't see for much longer.'

They passed the gun in the twilight. It seemed somehow neglected, left behind by the convoys, the martial tide flooding seawards. A damp figure kept vigil. 'Seen the mongrel?' It shrugged. The darkening tree-wall dripped quietly. They pulled up by the hutment.

'We'd never spot him,' Tuck grunted.

'I'm going to look.' Di got down.

They saw Sal come towards them. She eyed Tuck with foreboding and Di went to meet her, calling, 'Sal, have you seen him – we've lost the dog.'

Sal had halted. She was alone in the gloaming, a thin wet shape in the heather. 'You're too late.' Her face glistened. 'He went the same way as usual, like a sick fox, rump dragging.'

'Through the trees?'

'Half an hour back.'

'I'll find him,' Di blurted.

'No.' Her father grasped her elbow. 'Not by night in the forest. Let him go, his mind's settled.'

'We can't leave him.'

Tuck held her.

'Oh, Dad . . .'

His grasp tightened.

8

The dog dragged through the forest. Ancient trails of beasts scored it, paths of deer, tracks of badgers, but the mongrel ignored them. He took no heed of his surroundings, stumbling on through the growth, dark encumbering brush, thorns which scratched his flanks open, each step more demanding as his strength failed, dusk deepening.

A star shone. The dog rested.

One might have seen, while he paused, that his haunches were wasted, his coat in parts patchy. Pads, worn now like old car tyres, were hard, cracked and age-bleached. Eyes once bright gazed opaquely, orbs glazed. They stared dimly. Life ebbed. Yet he rallied. With a lurch, the dog shifted.

For a moment he teetered, glancing feebly behind, then continued the journey. Sheer stubbornness drove him. Now he fell, rolling sideways, lying dazed before rising. Now he stopped, breath expended. Again, reserves stirred the mongrel, dregs of strength forced by will-power, by one final compulsion, to carry him onward.

Where the stream sluiced, he tumbled. Bruised and drenched, he recovered, advancing half-blindly. Brambles snagged and he whined, a kind of moaning frustration. He took no steps to avoid them, plodding on, the barbs tearing. Tufts of hair were left on them. Near-insensate, he blundered on.

The moon was up when the plane loomed.

Somehow, the dog reached the wreckage. Somehow, his limbs had kept moving. Now, he dropped by an engine. To the owl on its hunt-path tight between the tree columns, the old farmdog looked froglike, head grounded, the feet splayed. Zac was spent, scarcely conscious.

Unimpressed, the owl passed and the dog, gulping grimly, crawled the last yards by inches. Beside the cockpit, he flopped. His trip was made. The dog sighed. The trees were still. He was peaceful a short while before he died.

Tuck did not sleep. Much of the night it was cloudy though once he saw starshine. Looking out of the window, he thought of the forest, its depths, and felt empty. He had an impulse to go there, shout for Zac. He went nowhere.

A calf bawled and Rose, restless, thought she heard the dog moving. She sat up.

'You were dreaming.'

She grunted.

Tuck listened. There was a low, far-off rumble. It was an hour after midnight. The rumbling lasted some minutes, died away then restarted. It came and went through the small hours, a growl like breakers on shingle, the sound of heavy planes passing.

He took a torch to the kitchen. Di was there with a candle, Rose's small kettle grumbling. 'Making tea.' The flame shuddered. Their shadows jumped. 'Haven't slept yet.' Her eyes were bleary.

'Damned airplanes.'

Di looked up. 'Yes – the airplanes.' The girl filled the teapot. 'I can't believe that he's gone, Dad.'

'Good old dog.'

'Yes.'

Tuck waited as the tea brewed, and remembered. 'You should have seen him at first ...' Zac had cringed in the parlour. He had lived rough in the woods and looked wild, cold and starving. '*A bag of bones,*' Rose had called him. He remembered their words.

'*We're not keeping him, Tuck.*'

'*Go on, fill him a bowl, Rose.*'

'*For tonight, then he's going.*'

Zac had fed like a shark, lips curled back, his teeth snapping. '*I'm not keeping a house dog,*' Rose had huffed, arms akimbo. '*He can stop for tonight, Tuck.*' It had, thought Tuck, been a long night. He lit an oil lamp and brooded.

When Di went up, the farmer lingered. He felt the teapot

much later – its contents were tepid. Rising, Tuck put on gumboots and reached for a topcoat. Outside, the air roused him. It was dark still but dry and he went to the box-shed.

He swung the torch. Nothing moved. In the barn, a rat scuttled. Hens were roosting. Tuck crossed the yard to the lean-to. He was aware it was futile but the farmer kept looking, knowing Zac would not be there, needing somehow to prove it.

On and off, he heard rumbling.

By now, dawn was approaching, a single bird singing. A great roar hushed the minstrel and Tuck was awed. The sound mounted. It seemed to swell from the darkness, to rise from the forest. Then, in the sky where light glimmered, he could see the armada.

'Rose!' He made for the house. 'Come and look!' he shouted.

She stumbled out in her nightclothes. Di was with her, hair tousled. As they watched, the air thundered and planes filled the heavens: straining tug-ships with gliders, fighter escorts above them. They came in streams, a dark pageant, everywhere the din blaring.

Rose put an arm round her daughter.

On black wings, the craft lumbered, like huge fowl, coastward flighting. Out to sea, warships wallowed and fleets of landing-boats surged. The dusky flocks flew above them. Since midnight, some had shuttled. Now they roared where the Tucks stood.

'Been four years,' Rose said quietly. 'Four years since Dunkirk, Tuck.'

He placed an arm with her own, the trio linked, staring upwards. 'Been a long time,' the man said.

Di said nothing.

The planes droned.

Wilf Tuck strode to the sheep. He had steadied the horses and could hear the ewes bleating. They were fraught, quick to huddle. 'Damned commotion,' Shep spluttered. 'Bloody planes!'

184

'Back to France, Shep.'

'Blamed war,' snarled the shepherd.

'It's the landing at last, man!'

'Scaring sheep ...'

Tuck smelled frying. The door of Shep's hut was open: a rich odour wafted. '*You're* all right,' growled the farmer, 'cooking breakfast – no danger!'

'I done *my* bit in the last lot.'

'Huh!' said Tuck. He was listening. The summer's dawn had grown silent. Then, in sudden eruption, fighter aircraft screamed over.

Shep howled at the running sheep. He sent his big dog to stop them. He said, 'A fine breakfast *I'll* have!'

'Where's the bitch?' Tuck demanded.

'You want to ask the damned mongrel!'

Tuck look fierce.

Shep said, 'Damn him!' He waved a claw at his shelter. 'Look in there. If I catch him ...'

'You're too late.'

Tuck peered grimly. It was grey in the hut and the sausages sizzling were black as the frying pan. He glanced into the corner. The sheepdog bitch lay on sacking, eyes watching him closely. The pups she nursed wriggled snugly. 'Zac's?' croaked Tuck.

'What do *you* think?'

'Aye,' the big man said softly. 'They'll be Zac's, Shep.'

Author's Note

Since interest in farming history is now widespread, I should perhaps mention that the farm scenes and descriptions in the preceding pages are based as well as I can remember on my experiences as a farm lad at the beginning of the war period.

At that time, the revolution in farm production, with all the headaches to come from it, had barely started. In Britain, there were still five heavy horses on the land for every tractor; farmers accustomed to £1 an acre profit on oats and barley were not impatient to grow more corn; while the only chemical sprayer I recall on a sizeable mixed farm was a small back-pack discharging through a hand-held nozzle. This spent most of its life in a tool shed.

Everywhere, as I remember, old ploughs and harrows lay under nettles. I seemed to be forever stumbling on these implements, half-buried in the corner of fields like ancient relics. It was a countryside then green with grasslands, hills and meadows undisturbed in many cases for centuries. It was still a countryside of haywains, of time-honoured hedgerows and tranquil lanes.

No one, in those days, had heard of a conservationist. Farmers – at least, those I remember – simply held it an article of faith that the land was held in trust for descendants and required to be maintained 'in good heart'. One gave back to the earth, I was often told, what one took from it. My tutors were neither aesthetes nor sentimentalists. They described wild flowers as 'weeds' – their meadows were bright with them. To such people, the slaughter of beasts was a fact of life, yet they regarded their livestock with a natural respect and would have despised 'factory farming'.

Of course there were callous farmers: most people knew and disapproved of them. The Tucks of my youth would not have slept easy with uncared-for animals and I recall bleary eyes at breakfast after nightlong vigils with ailing creatures. Like cavalrymen, good farmers put their beasts first, themselves second.

Much was changing and war gave the change dramatic impetus. Suddenly, under blockade, Britain needed to provide her own daily bread. The first call was to plough a million acres of grassland for cultivation. Soon, a second million followed, and a third. By 1942, more than 130,000 two- and three-furrow ploughs were at work, 'ploughing for victory'. Starvation was averted, agricultural output mounted and farmers were hailed as good fellows, almost heroes.

It would have been hard to guess, when survival seemed a miracle, that corn and butter mountains lay ahead – created at the expense of the very countryside for which so many, in those days, had gone to fight. But that is another story.

One change in the years to follow has always struck me as curious: the decline of the mongrel dog. When I was a boy, the dogs on farms and in villages were resourceful, countrywise, peripatetic and crossbred. By comparison, the thoroughbreds we sometimes saw with posh people seemed daft animals.

Today, everybody keeps thoroughbreds. I write this on a farm where stockmen, woodmen, tractor-drivers and gaffer alike keep pure-bred dogs and, I confess, my own are pedigree. They are not, I have learned, daft, but I still believe the mongrels of my youth were wiser. Zac, modelled on one or two I best remember, is by no means a 'wonder dog', just a good all-rounder, as farmers of the period would, I think, testify.

A R Lloyd
Kent
1985